T0147175

The Endearing Light

CECILE CZOBITKO

WESTBOW
PRESS®
A DIVISION OF THOMAS NELSON
& ZONDERVAN

WestBow Press books may be ordered through booksellers or by contacting:

WestBow Press
A Division of Thomas Nelson & Zondervan
1663 Liberty Drive
Bloomington, IN 47403
www.westbowpress.com
1 (866) 928-1240

ISBN: 978-1-9736-7671-3 (sc)
ISBN: 978-1-9736-7673-7 (hc)
ISBN: 978-1-9736-7672-0 (e)

Library of Congress Control Number: 2019915872

Print information available on the last page.

WestBow Press rev. date: 10/31/2019

I

I often wondered why my name was Trudy Rendell, while my mother's was Ellen Long. I well remembered the day I finally asked her why we had different last names. She sat me down and told me that I was only three years old when my father died in a car accident, leaving her to raise my three brothers and me all by herself.

My brothers were all older than me. Tony and Ryan were in their teens when our father died. Andy, the youngest of the three, was five years younger. When recalling my younger years, I could only remember Andy. I had no recollection of Tony and Ryan ever living with us. Mom said they left shortly after our father died.

My mother was a professional seamstress who made a living designing and sewing fancy dresses for weddings, graduations, proms, and other special occasions. While growing up, I often helped in her shop, doing odds and ends. What I liked most was when Mom used me as a live mannequin.

On one such occasion, while Mom was pinning a hem on the dress I wore, I asked her, "Why don't Tony and Ryan come to see us more often?"

She looked up at me and said, "Oh, I don't know. They have busy lives, I guess. Why do you ask?"

"I've been thinking about what Andy said the last time he was here. About how Tony never comes to see us. Why is that?" I answered.

Mom gave a sigh as she got up.

"Well, Trudy, after your dad died, we had very hard days," she said. "All we had to live on was what I took in from my sewing and the small amount the boys brought in. There wasn't enough to pay all the bills, so I decided to rent out the basement room. That was Tony's room at the time. It caused a big problem because Tony, the eldest, did not want to move out of his room and share a room with his two younger brothers. Tony figured he was the man of the house. He was eighteen and out of school. He was bringing home some money from the job he had, so he thought he should be the one to make the decisions. When I told him that we needed more money to make ends meet, he got very upset with me."

Mom paused as she looked to see if the hem she had pinned fell the right way. Then, she continued, "Things got even worse when I rented the room to John. Tony made it known that he did not like John and tried to get his brothers to join in with him. He was so rude to John that I sometimes could have slapped his face. But I never understood the reason why he was behaving like he was. Finally, I realized it was because he was hurting and missed his father."

She finished pinning the hem and told me to take the dress off.

After I handed the dress to Mom, I asked, "So what made him move out?"

My mother did not answer; she just shook her head.

I could see that what had happened years ago was still a very sensitive issue. I sat beside her and put my hand on her arm. "Sorry I asked, Mom. It's okay if you don't want to tell me."

"Trudy, there are feelings that never go away. You were so little when your dad died. I tried so hard to make a good home for us, but Tony never saw it that way. To his reasoning the house was his father's, and no other man was welcome to live in it. He even accused me of being unfaithful to his father. We had a bitter argument, he packed his things and left home the next day," Mom said, wiping away a tear that had rolled down her cheek. She looked at me and then continued, "He never told me where he was going.

For a month I worried about him. It wasn't until I called my brother on his birthday, that I found out Tony was living with him. I was so relieved to know where Tony was, I never bothered to ask why he had never let me know."

I hugged Mom and said, "Well, I think you took care of us very well. I don't really remember Dad, but I remember feeling that something had changed. Maybe what I sensed was that Dad was not with us anymore, but John was. How long was it before you and John got together?"

That made my mother smile. "Oh, Trudy, you sure are inquisitive today. Well, with the rent John was paying and the odd jobs Ryan did, we settled into a new normal. After your other two brothers finished school, they left home, leaving just you and me. John started to stay longer after eating supper, or he would ask if I wanted to see a movie with him. After a while, I started to miss him when he was away. So, after two years of courting, five years after your dad died, we decided to get married."

"I remember when you got married; it's one of my best recollections. I was seven, soon to be eight. I remember being very happy to wear the beautiful white dress you had made for me."

"Yes, and do you remember when we moved to the city?"

"Yes, I remember. I was so scared; everything was so different. There were so many houses in the city! I was scared to leave home because, if I did, I might not find the house again. Another thing that I remember was being left with a babysitter. That probably scared me even more," I replied, remembering the awful girl who babysat me.

Mom gave me a small smile and said, "I never realized you felt that way. You never said anything; you didn't even cry when I left you. I'm sorry for that."

"It's okay, Mom. I think it's just part of growing up." I looked at the time and said, "I told Joan I'd babysit tonight. Is John going to be home?"

"No, he's not due back till next week," Mom replied, rubbing her eyes.

"Oh, I thought he was going to be back tonight. I don't like leaving you by yourself. Maybe I should call Joan and tell her I can't make it."

"No, Trudy, don't do that. Joan told me she was going to a party to see her husband get an award. It's too late to tell her you can't make it."

"Okay, but you know how I hate to miss my time with you. I better go get something to eat. Do you want me to make something for you?"

"No, dear, I want to finish this dress before I eat. You go ahead. I'll be fine."

"Mom, I think you should take a break. When was the last time you ate?" I asked, concerned because Mom often worked long hours, forgetting to eat and to take care of herself.

"Okay, Trudy, I'll come have a quick bite," Mom said.

We went to the kitchen together. After I made her a sandwich, she quickly ate it and then returned to her work, leaving me on my own.

As I ate my sandwich, I thought about my relationship with John. He was a long-haul truck driver. Those hauls usually took him away from home for two weeks at a time. When he returned, he and Mom liked to have time to themselves, so I made myself scarce. When he was gone, I'd have my mom to myself again. He never let me call him Dad, but he provided for me like one. He never corrected me but would tell my mother when he thought I had done something wrong. John was very disciplined and expected me to be also. He disliked it when I left my stuff lying around and did not clean up after myself.

One thing that Mom and I disagreed with was John's belief that there was no God. He said that religion was just for the weak. If there was a God, why was the world in this kind of state? Before mom married John, she would send me to Sunday school, but when we moved to the city she never did.

I was in my last year of high school, looking forward to graduation, which was only days away. I was very fond of this guy in my English class. When he asked me to be his date for grad, I said yes, hardly able to control my enthusiasm. Finn was tall and very charming. He was very popular with the kids at school; they liked to be around him. I thought that he was the handsomest guy at school.

My mother had been working on my grad dress all month, but I had not seen it. I had asked many times to see it, but Mom just kept telling me to be patient. She wanted it to be a surprise, so she made me wait until she had it finished. With Finn as my escort and the beautiful dress Mom was making for me, I knew that my grad was going to be just like I had always dreamed it would be.

With two days left before the grad, I asked, "Mom, can I see the dress tonight?"

"Well, I suppose. You will have to see it eventually," she answered.

We made our way to her sewing room, and when we got there, she made me close my eyes as she went to take the cover off the mannequin that was wearing my dress. When I opened my eyes, I saw the most beautiful dress! The color was so special. The top of the dress was a light pink with the color gradually turning to a deep red at the bottom of the dress. It was a princess-style dress, with tiny pleats that went from the left shoulder diagonally across to the right side at the waist. At the waist, the pleats continued all the way down the one side of the skirt.

When I admired myself in the mirror, I saw that the dress fit my slender frame perfectly, making me look even taller. The red in the dress brought out my strawberry-blonde hair.

"Oh, Mom, this dress is so beautiful! You've outdone yourself! Thank you so much!" I exclaimed, giving her a huge hug.

"I'm glad you like it. You do look very pretty in it. I was a little concerned that you would not like the color," Mom said as she came over to see how the hem fell.

"Oh, not at all, Mom; it's just perfect," I replied. I gave Mom another hug, and as I stepped back, I saw her flinch and touch her head. I held on to her and said, "Are you all right? What's the matter?"

"Oh, it's nothing—just a little pain above my eye," Mom replied.

On graduation day my mom did my hair and makeup and helped me with the dress.

When Finn came to my house to pick me up, I introduced him to my parents. I was very surprised to see how shy he was in front of my mother and John. He greeted them politely and gave me a red-rose corsage. After my mom pinned it to the dress, Finn and I left for the grad.

As we were walking to his car, Finn said, "Trudy, you look like a princess. That dress is very lovely."

"Thank you, Finn. And you look very handsome in that tux," I replied as he helped me into the car.

Grad was quite an affair, with a delicious meal followed by a formal dance. We had a live band that played a wide range of music, from good oldies to current tunes. Although I was not a very good dancer, I enjoyed dancing with Finn. We did not stop dancing until the music stopped for the night. After the dance, we were invited to a beach party the grads were giving, but we only stayed a short time because I got so cold, all I could do was shiver.

Finn brought me home, and when we were on the front steps, he brought me close and kissed me.

After the kiss, he said, "Trudy, I had a really good time. I'll call you. Good night."

"Yes, Finn, it was fun. I'd like that. Good night," I said and then went into the house.

Finn never called. I later learned that he had left town for the summer to work on a paving crew.

Life went on. I applied to a local college to attend an early childhood education course. I wanted to become a kindergarten teacher. I loved little kids, and when I got a summer job working as an assistant to help run a summer day camp for preschoolers, I couldn't have been happier. A week into the summer, I arrived home to find my mother crying. When she saw me, she tried to hide her tears, but she knew I had seen them.

When I came closer to her, I saw that she looked very pale.

"Mom, what is the matter? Why are you crying?" I asked.

For a while she did not say anything; she just sat on the couch, looking at me.

Then, with her hands shaking, she patted the couch and said, "Trudy, come sit by me."

I did as she asked.

"Oh, I don't know how I can tell you this." She reached for me, wrapping her arms around me, and said, "Well, as you know, I've been having bad headaches for the last month. I went for tests last week, and today I went to see the doctor for the results. It's not good. The doctor found a growth in my brain. I have brain cancer— the type not very many survive. He said I have only a year to live."

Mom covered her face with her hands and started to cry.

"Oh, Mom," I said as I put my arms around her and held her until she stopped crying.

I could not find any words to comfort her. It felt like someone had punched me in the stomach. I just held my mom, as if by doing so it would make her all better. *Oh! Where are my brothers, and where is John?* I felt so frightened, and as I thought about Mom being sick, I started to cry.

"Please don't say anything to the boys; I want to tell them myself," Mom said, then, more to herself than to me, she added, "Oh, how am I going to tell this to John? He was so looking forward to our future, with just the two of us."

I was in shock. *How can this be happening to Mom? Oh, please, not my mom!*

I wiped away my tears and asked, "Did the doctor say there were any treatments for the cancer?"

"The doctor said I could try chemo, but he doesn't think it will help. This type of cancer is very aggressive, and he has not seen many who have survived it," Mom replied.

"Mom, how are you feeling now? Are you in any pain?"

"I just have a slight headache. The doctor gave me some painkillers, so I feel okay right now," Mom replied, then continued, "I have an appointment at the cancer clinic tomorrow. John will be back tonight. He can come with me. I really don't know how I am going to tell him this."

I could see how frightened she was.

"I could come with you," I offered.

"Oh no. You have the little kids to care for," Mom replied.

That was just like my mom, always concerned for others, always putting everyone else before herself.

For the remainder of the summer I continued to work with the kids. Most days, Mom seemed fine, but I could tell she was growing weaker. When I received my acceptance to college, I decided not to attend, but Mom would not hear of it. When I first applied, I was looking forward to attending college, but now Mom's health gave me great concern. John tried to be home more, but he had a trucking contract; if he failed to meet the contract's terms, he would not be paid. Mom kept her business going, but by the end of the summer, she stopped doing the fine details on gowns because she said it bothered her eyes. She still designed the dresses, but she left the sewing to the woman she had hired.

Once I was in college, John talked Mom into coming with him on a haul, but they soon found that the traveling only made the pain in her head worse. Although he hated to leave Mom alone, he had to keep on working. I'd go to college in the morning and return in the late afternoon. When John was away, I was Mom's only caregiver. I saw Mom's ability to concentrate gradually decline, and she would easily get frustrated. Early in the new year, when I returned home one day, I found Mom lying down in the dark; she said the light made the pain in her head worse. That was the first time I realized just how sick Mom was. I hated leaving Mom alone and was thinking of dropping out of school, but Mom said she wanted me to keep going. Oh, how I wished the school year would end, but it just dragged on. When it finally did end, Mom took a turn for the worse.

I was so thankful that I was done with school because Mom's cancer progressed very rapidly. She could not care for herself any longer and needed twenty-four-hour care. Mom now spent most of her time in a dark room because light caused her even more pain.

John had been gone for two weeks. I found the responsibility of being the sole caregiver for Mom, overwhelming. One day, after I had settled Mom for her afternoon nap, there was a knock on the front door. I went to the door, expecting some person selling magazines, but there before me stood a well-dressed woman.

"Hello, I'm Mary. You must be Trudy," she said.

"Yes, what can I do for you?" I asked. I wasn't in a good mood and did not want to talk to anyone.

"I'm here to see if I can help you. I know that your mother is sick. I have come to see if you need any help," Mary said.

It took me a few seconds to realize what she was saying.

"Yes, I do need help, but I don't know you," I replied, feeling some tears welling up in my eyes.

"Trudy, I got to know your mother when she designed a dress for my daughter three years ago. You might remember my daughter. Her name is Alicia."

"You're Alicia's mom? Of course, I remember her. I've been so worried; I just can't think straight anymore," I said, relieved that I could accept Mary's offer of assistance.

"Is there anything I could do now?" Mary asked.

"Oh, it would be so helpful if you could stay with Mom while I go do some shopping. John has been delayed getting home. We're getting very low on food."

"Yes, I can stay with your Mom. Go do what you need to do; I can stay for as long as it takes," Mary said.

When I showed Mary to Mom's room, Mom was sleeping peacefully, so Mary went to sit on the chair beside her bed. After thanking Mary, I left for the grocery store. When I returned and had put all the groceries away, I went to check on mom. To my surprise, Mom was awake and sitting up in bed. Something was different about her. Was that a smile I saw?

Mary had a book in her hands, and when she closed it, I saw that it was a Bible. Before I could say that we did not believe in that book, Mary stood up and said, "That did not take you very long. Is there anything else I can do for you?"

"No, I can manage now. Thank you so much for your help," I answered.

Mary put her hand in her pocket, pulled out a piece of paper, and handed it to me, saying, "Here's my number. Please call me if you need more help. I live just around the corner."

I was going to tell Mary we did not need any more help, but I heard Mom try to say something.

"Would you like Mary to return?" I asked Mom.

Mom nodded her head, so Mary agreed to come take care of Mom twice a week. The days Mary came were like a breath of fresh air. It always made Mom happy when Mary came to be with her. I was able to go shopping for what we needed and do things for myself. When I returned, I often heard Mary reading to Mom from the Bible. I knew that this would not please John, so I left that little part out when I told him that Mary was coming to help. He was glad that I had help, but when he was home, he took care of Mom.

As the weeks went by Mom got even worse. Her eyesight slowly diminished until she became blind. She became so weak, she stopped speaking. Then, the day came when she was not able to swallow, so it was decided that she go to a hospice. John and I hated to see Mom in a place like that, but we knew she was getting better care there than we could give her at home. In the months before her death one of us was always with Mom; we never left her alone.

The day Mom died, Mary and I were by her bedside. Mary was reading when Mom suddenly raised her arm—something she had not done in a while—took Mary's hand, and placed it over her heart.

Then, Mom looked at me, squeezed my hand, and tried to smile. She closed her eyes and stopped breathing.

Just like that, Mom had left us. I suddenly felt so alone. Big tears started to roll down my cheeks, and I cried, "Mom, you can't go; I need you." I laid my head on her hand and sobbed.

I felt Mary close beside me. She rubbed my back and said, "Trudy, your mom is now with Jesus. He will take care of her. Don't worry; we will see her again one day."

When I heard that, I said, "Why would God take her from us? Why didn't God heal her? Maybe John is right. Maybe there is no God."

Mary smiled and said, "Trudy, just trust and believe. I know how hurt you are now, but just trust."

It suddenly occurred to me that I needed to tell John about Mom. John had gone for a short trip but had been delayed because of a traffic accident.

"I've got to phone John," I said as I pushed past Mary and went to find my phone.

The minute John heard my voice, he yelled, "Is it Ellen? Has she passed?"

I could not say anything, but, somehow, he knew. "I'm just about home, Trudy. I'll take care of your mother. Don't you worry."

Ryan and Andy came home for the funeral John had arranged for Mom. We were standing by Mom's grave when Mary came to stand by me. She said she had come to say goodbye to her friend.

Mary asked John if she could read a passage from the Bible, but John said, "No. Ellen never believed in that kind of stuff."

Mary smiled at him and replied, "Ellen was a believer, John. She is now in heaven, looking down on us."

Mary then smiled at the rest of us, turned, and walked away.

During the period when Mom was sick, John became more cynical. He had tried to be there for Mom, but he could not make her well.

Mom passed exactly a year after she had been diagnosed. After my mother died, my reason to live died also. All was black; nothing made any sense anymore.

A few days after the funeral, I was going through my mother's things when I found a garment bag with a note pinned to it. It read, 'Trudy, I made this dress for you, my dear daughter. I had so hope to see you wear it on your wedding day. Love Mom.' For a few seconds I just stared at the bag, trying to comprehend what my mother had done for me. At the thought of it, sorrow engulfed me. The thought of opening the bag to see the dress, was unbearable, I just collapsed on the floor and started to cry.

2

As the months passed, I became more and more depressed. I missed my mother and wanted her to be with me. I felt so alone in this world. I had no friends, no job, and no education, and I had no ambition of getting any of them. I spent my days watching TV and cried myself to sleep every night. I knew I was spiraling down into a deep depression but did not know how to get out.

After Mom died, John would take long trips and be gone for weeks at a time, leaving me home alone.

When he returned from one of these trips, he found the house a mess and went ballistic.

"Trudy, clean up this mess! What do you do all day?" he said angrily.

I had never seen him so upset. I got off the couch and went to clean the kitchen, afraid that if I didn't, he'd ask me to leave his house.

As I cleaned, he came to sit at the table and said, "Why don't you go out and see your friends? It's not good for you to stay here all day by yourself."

"I have no friends," I replied. With that realization, I started to cry.

When John saw the tears, he just let me be. Looking back now, I don't think he knew what to do for me. I finished cleaning and returned to the movie I had been watching.

That night, when I was in bed, I heard a knock on my bedroom door. It was John, saying something I could not make out. Then, I heard him say, "I need you, Trudy."

Thinking that he was in trouble, I ran to the door to find John leaning against the door frame. He grabbed me and started to kiss me. I was so shocked, I didn't say a word. I quickly got away from him, rushed back into my room, and slammed the door. I stood against the door, unable to believe what just had happened. When I heard John's bedroom door close, I went back to bed but could not fall asleep.

When John came staggering into the kitchen the following morning, I did not look up at him or say anything to him. I just played with the cereal in my bowl, waiting for him to say something.

He made himself a cup of instant coffee and came to sit at the table, not saying a word.

Finally, unable to keep quiet any longer, I said, "What was that all about last night?"

"What about last night?" he asked, taking a sip of coffee.

"Are you still so drunk that you don't remember? You knocked on my door, saying you needed me. Then, you grabbed me and kissed me."

"Oh, that!" he replied. He did not say anything else; he just looked at me the way he always did when I was a little girl. I knew that he loved me as a daughter and last night, it was the liquor that had made him behave the way he had.

But then. I heard him say, "I need a woman in my life, and since you're here, it might as well be you. I want you to share my bed."

Left speechless, I thought, *What is wrong with you? Have you lost your mind?*

Then, he continued, "If you are not willing to do that, you'll have to leave my house today."

I sat there, unsure I had heard him right, so I asked, "What? You want me to do what? Why are you saying these things to me?" I stood up and then continued, "You must still be drunk. You can't be serious! How can you say these things to me? You're my father! Mother would be horrified."

I started to walk out of the room when I heard him say, "You can have your mother's car and this bank draft for ten thousand dollars."

I stopped and looked at him. The look in his face told me he was dead serious.

"Where would I go?" I asked, realizing that I had no option but to go.

"Go anywhere you want to go. Just get in the car and drive away. I'm going to see if my truck is ready, and when I get back this afternoon, I want you gone. You can take anything you want but remember that you have to be gone," John replied.

I was in shock. John had thrown me out. I was so angry with him, it made me want to leave. I took a shower, then I got dressed in my jeans and a sweater I had not worn since Mom got sick. Feeling discouraged and angry, I packed everything in my room, even the curtains and matching bedspread. I was also mindful to take the special dress mom had made for me. I did not want to leave anything that showed that I had ever lived there. I went to my mother's room and took her jewelry box and the boxes of pictures. Once I had all my things in the car, I went to make myself something to eat. After I finished eating, I left the kitchen a mess, even leaving the milk on the table, for I knew that this would upset John. I hurried; there was no way I wanted to be there when John returned. If I never saw that man again it would be too soon.

Before I left, I wrote him a note: "I always thought you were a nice man until today. You turned out to be the most dreadful person I have ever known. I hope to never see you again." Signed, "Once your daughter."

Before I left town, I went to the ATM to deposit the bank draft, then I drove to the cemetery to say goodbye to Mom. At the cemetery, the sun was shining, and the little birds were happily singing their sweet songs.

It's such a beautiful day, and yet this is where my mother is buried. How can this possibly make sense? I thought.

Sitting by her grave, I noticed the flowers. They must have been from John, for they were lilies, my mother's favorite flower. They were the only flowers he had ever given her. As I sat there, I found it very difficult to find the words I wanted to say. Finally, I told her that I was leaving but did not know where I would end up. I told her that I loved her and missed her desperately. Big tears came to my eyes. Why did mom have to leave me? Why?

I wiped the tears off my face and returned to the car. As I left the main road, leading out of town, I came to an intersection. I had to decide which way I should go, left or right. I was drawn to turn right, to go south. I put the right signal light on, and when the traffic cleared, I stepped on the gas and drove in that direction.

B

As I drove, my thoughts turned to my family, such as it was. I did not have much of a family anymore. My mother was gone, and my dad had passed away years before. I had three brothers I could go see. But I didn't really know them; besides, they had gone on with their lives. Tony left home when I was just a little girl and had come home only a few times after that. He had not even called once to see how Mom was doing and did not bother to come to the funeral. I would not be welcome there; he would be much too busy to see me. I knew Ryan a little better, but he had just quit the air force and was moving to a new place. Andy was overseas. He had come home for Mom's funeral and then returned to his post immediately. I was on my own. I had to find my own place.

I drove until the gas gauge showed the tank was almost empty. I had not stopped once. I needed to take a break and find a place to spend the night. As I drove a little farther, I saw a sign in the distance. When I got closer, I was thankful to see Hope Motel and a service station. I fueled up the car, then drove to the motel. I stopped in front of the office sign and went in. The woman at the front desk had me fill in the registration card and asked how I'd be paying. After I handed her the money, she gave me the key.

Before I left to go to my room, I asked, "Is there any restaurant around here?"

"Oh yes. We have a restaurant downstairs; it will be open until ten. We also offer room service, if you'd like to eat in your room," she replied.

Once I was in the room, the bed looked so inviting that I just collapsed on it. As I lay on the bed, I could see the motel sign flashing, "Hope, Hope." It occurred to me that there was no hope. Mary had talked about the blessed hope, but I knew nothing about that. John had always said that you made your own way in this world and depending on anything other than yourself was worthless. With that thought, I just broke down; big sobs coursed through me. I don't know how long I cried, but I must have fallen asleep for a while. When I woke up, it was dark in my room. I checked the time and saw that it was eight o'clock. I suddenly felt hungry.

I was going to order room service, but then I decided to go to the restaurant and have a meal there. I went to the bathroom, splashed water on my face, and combed my fingers through my hair. I looked like a mess, but I was too hungry to mind.

When I entered the restaurant, the waitress promptly sat me in a booth overlooking the courtyard of the motel. I ordered a hamburger and fries, and as I waited, I looked at the newspaper that had been left on the table. There wasn't very much of interest in the paper, but then an ad caught my eye. Someone was looking for a nanny for his boys. The ad said the position was opened to someone who would love working with a special-needs kid.

Now this is interesting. I could be a nanny; I've always wanted to care for kids, I thought.

Then, as I read the end of the ad, there was an email address to apply for the position. I reached for my purse to get my phone, but found it wasn't there, in my rush to leave, I must have forgotten to take it. Now this was a problem, with no phone I would not be able to apply.

When I got my food, I asked the waitress if she knew about this position. She said that she did not but the people who ran the motel might. I thanked her and attacked the food before me.

When I went to bed that night, I thought about what it would mean *if I got that job. I could have my own money and not use John's money. I didn't want to live on his dime. I'd keep that money for emergencies.* I liked that; it made me feel good. I suddenly realized that maybe there was some hope after all; a little glimmer of light in the darkness. The darkness tried to take hold again, but I held on to that little glimmering light. I was starting a new life, and I somehow knew there was no place for this darkness anymore.

In the morning I went to the motel office to inquire about the ad. As I checked out, I asked the woman at the counter, "Would you know about this ad?"

"Yes, that's Richard's ad. He's looking for a nanny for his boys," she replied.

"I'd like to apply, but I don't have my phone. Would you have a way to get a hold of him?" I asked.

She smiled and said, "Tell you what. I'll call him myself. If the position is not filled, I'll let you talk to him. Will that be all right with you?"

"Yes, of course, thank you," I replied.

As she made the call, I thought, *It's so very odd to talk to a stranger and ask him if I could be a nanny to his kids. What do I say? "Take me; I can be your kids' nanny? Trust me."*

I was deep in thought when the woman asked, "What's your name? Richard wants to know."

After I told her my name, she handed me the phone.

"Hello," I said very reluctantly.

"Hello, Trudy. I'm Richard. Shelly is a good judge of character, and if she's calling me for you, she must think you're okay. The position is still open. I'll interview you. When can you come to my place?" the man named Richard said.

"I could be there anytime you want. Just tell me where you live," I answered.

"It's not too hard to get here. Turn right as you leave the motel and right again at the four-way stop. Keep going for about twelve miles, and you'll get to a gate. There's a buzzer on the gate. Ring it and wait until Tex comes for you. He'll let you in and lead you to the house."

I repeated his directions, and when he said I had them right, I thanked him for giving me an interview.

As I handed the phone back to Shelly, I suddenly realized that the little light had become a bit brighter.

As I drove to this far-off place, I wondered just what I was getting into.

The woman at the motel knows Richard. After all, this seems like a nice community where people know one another. It will be okay, I convinced myself.

After a while I came to the gate Richard had described. It was a metal gate with metal broncos on each side of it. At the top of the gate was a design of an open-loop lasso with the end of the rope going down to form an L. I got out of the car, rang the buzzer, and waited.

It suddenly struck me as strange to be doing what I was doing.

Do I really want this? What in the world am I thinking? Why did I agree to come here? I thought.

As I waited, I looked around. There was an older-looking house a little way up the road, with beautiful big trees surrounding it. Across the road from the old house was a stand of large pine trees. In the distance there were rolling hills covered with evergreen trees. Just in front of me was a large field; there must have been more than a hundred cows grazing on it. I wondered where the house and other buildings on this ranch were, and then I heard a vehicle coming toward me. As it stopped in front of me, I saw a cowboy get off his quad. He was a real cowboy with cowboy boots and cowboy hat; all that was missing was his horse. I felt like I had step into a western movie.

The man walked toward me and said he was Tex. He was an older-looking man; he reminded me of John Wayne.

He came to the gate and said, "Hi, miss. You must be Trudy."

I nodded.

He gave me a big smile and pushed the gate open.

"Go on in and wait till I close the gate, then you can follow me up to the house," he instructed.

The driveway curved to the right, around the trees. As I rounded the curve, I saw a huge log house nestled in the pine trees. The path that led to the front door was hedged by beautiful dark red dahlias in full bloom. A short distant from the house there were buildings and corrals.

As I sat in my car, admiring my surroundings, I thought, *This is a very big house. It must be for a big family. I wonder how many kids live here.*

I got out of the car, walked to the door, and rapped the big brass door knocker.

I waited for a short time, then a tall, dark-haired, very handsome, well-built man answered the door. He had such deep-green eyes, I just could not stop staring at him. It wasn't until the man cleared his throat that I noticed what I was doing.

"Trudy, I assume?" he asked.

I suddenly felt very small. I tried to find my voice, but those eyes of his were so beautiful, all I could do was stare. I finally looked away, and as my face turned beet red, I said, "Yes. I'm Trudy."

When he smiled and I saw those dimples, I thought I was in love.

"Hi, I'm Richard Lance. Please come in," he said, still smiling.

I was so embarrassed, I could not look at him. I stepped inside the house and found myself in a large foyer. The foyer had three arches. The archway to the left led to two sets of stairs—one set going up, and the other going down. The archway to the right led to the kitchen and a large dining room. The middle archway was closed off by French doors. I supposed the living room would be behind those doors.

Richard led me to his study downstairs and asked if I wanted anything to drink. I asked for water. After he returned with a glass of water, Richard asked me to sit in a chair in front of his desk.

"You are not from around here. Where are you from?" he asked.

I became very uneasy. *Oh, why did I agree to do this? He's never going to hire me.*

"I'm from Quesnel, north of here. I needed something different, so I came here to look for work. I always wanted to work with children, so when I saw your ad, I thought I'd apply. This is the first time I've applied for any work," I said.

Oh, this is going to make him want to hire me! I reproached myself.

"Have you taken care of children before?" Richard asked.

"Well, I've babysat, and I worked with kids in a day camp for one summer. I took a course in early childhood education at the local college, but I did not finish—because of family problems," I replied.

Richard smiled again. This made me so nervous. Why was he smiling?

"Taking care of a little boy with special needs is more than just babysitting."

"Oh, I know that. What kind of special needs does your son have?"

"Ned can be very destructive; he has big fits if he doesn't get his way. I must tell you before we go on, I've had four nannies for Ned in the last year. They all quit because they could not handle him," Richard replied.

"How old is your son?"

"He's five years old. He just started school," Richard said and then added, "Today my neighbor Liz is picking him up from school so that he can play with her son. I'll call and ask her to bring him home. If Ned likes you, the job is yours. But be warned: Ned is a very difficult little boy."

As I sat waiting for Ned to come home, I started to think about the situation. *This little boy is only five. How mean can he be? He can't be that bad. At least I hope not.*

"What was it that led you to look for work here?" Richard asked, interrupting my thoughts.

I sat for a few seconds without answering. I did not know if I should tell him about my mother.

But, a moment later, I found myself saying, "I cared for my mother for the past year. She was very sick and died this spring. I had to get away from home but did not know where I should go. I got in my car and just drove all day until I got here."

It surprised me that I had said all that without tearing up.

"I'm very sorry to hear that, Trudy. It must have been hard on you," Richard commented.

I did not want to answer any more questions about myself, so I said, "This is a lovely place you have. How long have you lived here?"

"This is a family ranch. I grew up here. My father started the ranch and named it the Open Lasso Ranch. We raise horses and cattle, supplying stock for rodeos all over western Canada. I work for the Rodeo Association. Most of the time, I work here on the ranch, but I often have to go to meetings in town."

Just as Richard finished answering my question, the door burst open, and a little boy ran in.

"Daddy!" he cried, then came to an abrupt stop in front of me. He became very quiet and looked up at me.

I was very surprised to see such a beautiful child. After all the things Richard had told me, I had envisioned a little monster. I stood up and bent down to the boy's level. Putting my hands on both sides of his face I said, "My, you have to be the most wonderful little boy I have ever seen. You have the loveliest green eyes, just like your father." I gave him a little kiss on the forehead and stood up. When I realized what I had just done my face turned bright red.

"Daddy is this lady going to be my nanny?" the little boy asked.

"Well, Ned, this is Miss Trudy Rendell. She's here to apply to be your nanny. Will you be nice to her?" Richard asked.

Just then, I noticed a lady standing in the doorway.

Richard stood up, went to the door, and said, "Liz, come in. I'd like to introduce you to Trudy Rendell. Trudy, this is Liz, the neighbor I told you about."

I went to shake Liz's hand and said, "Hello. It's nice to meet you, Liz."

"Daddy, we have to get Trudy for my nanny," Ned interrupted.

"I'll be good; I promise. I'll eat all my food, and I promise I will not make any messes. Please, Dad. Please."

"Well, we will leave the decision to Trudy," Richard said, then, turning to me, he went on to say, "Trudy, you heard what Ned said. What do you say?"

But before I could answer, Liz said, "I think Trudy would be a good fit here. But it's only my opinion. I've got to be going. Bye, Ned."

After she had gone, Richard asked, "Well, Trudy, what do you say?"

I looked at Ned and felt that this was where I was supposed to be, so I replied, "I'm willing to give it a try."

"Oh good! Trudy, come with me. I'll show you where the nannies stay." Ned was so happy, he came to take my hand and pulled me up the stairs.

Ned led me to the kitchen. As I entered the room, I found that the living room and the dining room were separated by a stone wall with a large wood fireplace built in it. In the front of the fireplace was a huge table with several chairs around it. On the back wall were patio doors that led to a covered deck. Ned led me to the patio doors and outside to a door that opened to a small apartment. The apartment looked very cozy, with a living room, bathroom, and bedroom. It did not have much furniture, just a bed and dresser in the bedroom and a couch and coffee table, with a small TV on it, in the living room.

As I looked around, I thought, *Once I have all my things in here, it'll feel like home.*

Richard had followed us. When he entered the apartment, he said, "As you can see, there is not much furniture here now. I just had the place painted. I have new furniture coming. Ned, I must talk to Trudy for a little while. Let's go back in the house; you can watch your show while we talk."

When we returned to the house, Ned went to watch his show, while Richard and I went to sit at the dining room table.

"There are a few things I have to go over with you," Richard said.

"Yes, of course. I have questions I'd like to ask too," I replied.

"Let me go first," he said. "Maybe those questions will be answered. Okay?"

I nodded, so he continued, "Ned has a big brother, Roger. He's nine. You'll have to care for him also."

"Oh yes. All right," I answered.

Richard went through all the things he wanted me to do. Then, he went over all the information I would need to care for the boys. I would be responsible for the boys Monday through Friday and have the weekend off. For formality's sake, Richard asked for some references and my permission to do a background check. I gave him the names of the lady I had babysat for and the name of the summer-camp coordinator. He was okay with me starting before those came in. I would be paid a monthly salary and have free room and board.

"Trudy, welcome to our home. I hope all will work out this time," Richard said.

"Yes, Mr. Lance, I hope so too. Thank you for trusting me," I said as I saw the little light shining even brighter.

"Call me Richard. You are part of the family, and no one is formal here. I think we went over most of the things you need to know. Do you have any other questions? Oh, before I forget, what is your phone number?" he asked.

"I don't have a phone, I forgot to take it when I left home," I replied feeling a little foolish.

"Don't you worry, I'll get you one. Now do you have any questions?" he asked again.

When I said no, he asked, "Would it be all right if I left the boys with you for a few hours tonight? I have to go meet someone."

"Yes, I think so. What time will you be going?" I asked.

"Oh, after supper. I'll have supper with the boys, then I'll go. Right now, it's time to go pick up Roger from soccer practice. Ned, come. We can show Trudy the way to school and introduce her to your teacher," Richard said.

4

As we drove to school, Ned gave me the play by play of the surrounding scenery. We arrived at this small hamlet, which consisted of the school, a general store, and a small library-museum on one side of the street, and four houses on the other side.

As we were getting out of the Jeep, Ned said, "This place is called Lanceville. Right, Dad?"

"Yes, Ned," Richard said. He then explained, "Trudy, my father donated the land and built the school because he thought that it was too far to send little kids all the way to the next town. We have classes from kindergarten to eighth grade. After that, the kids go to school in town, forty minutes from here. Later on, we subdivided the land surrounding the school and sold lots to the people who work near the hamlet."

As we entered the school, Roger was waiting for us. Ned ran to him and with much enthusiasm said, "Roger, Roger, guess what? We have a new nanny, she's very nice. She's not old like the ones before."

Roger gave him a look of disbelief and said, "Oh really? How long will it be before you make her go away?"

"I won't make her go away! I promised to be good," Ned said as I went to stand beside him. He turned to me and said, "Trudy, this is my big brother, Roger." Then, he turned to Roger and said, "This is Trudy, our new nanny. She's nice, don't you think?"

"Hi, it's nice to meet you Trudy. I hope Ned keeps his promise.

It's hard to get used to someone new every few months," Roger said as we shook hands.

"Well, Ned promised to be good," Richard said. "You two, go to the Jeep. I want to introduce Trudy to your teachers."

When we got back to the house, Richard went to the kitchen, so I followed. As we entered the kitchen, I noticed large pantry doors on the wall to the right. The kitchen was open to the dining room, separated by a large island. There was a long counter that ran the length of the kitchen and continued around the corner to the width of it. A sink was in the middle of that length, right below the window that faced the front of the house. In the island was an oversized cook stove.

Richard showed me around the kitchen, and when he opened the pantry doors, I discovered that it was a walk-in cooler stocked full of food.

"Wow, you sure have a lot of food!" I exclaimed.

"We keep a lot of food because I have ranch hands to feed," Richard replied. He went in and took out a casserole from one of the shelves. Then, he said, "Would you get that salad bowl and the salad dressing over there?"

I did, then walked out of the cooler and set the bowl on the counter.

"We just have to pop this casserole in the microwave and then supper will be ready," he said.

As we waited for the casserole to warm up, he asked, "Do you cook?"

"Yes, a little. When I was taking care of my mother, I was the one who prepared all the meals. Who made that casserole for you?"

"I have a cook who comes in every morning to prepare the food for the ranch. She will be here tomorrow morning. She made this for us this morning."

"Will I have to help her with the meals?"

"No. I hired you to take care of the boys."

"Okay, but I'm willing to cook for them. I'd like to have them help me. Would that be all right?"

"Sure, you can do that if you want; the kitchen is all yours," he answered and went to see if the casserole was warm enough.

After the boys helped me set the table, we all sat down to have supper. But before we could start, they all joined hands, and Richard said a blessing. This distressed me a little, but I went along with it.

As I served myself, I noticed that this casserole was made for ranch hands and not really suited for little boys. I watched Ned struggle to eat it.

After he ate most of the food on his plate, he asked, "Dad, I'm full. Is it okay if I don't eat the rest? I think I took too much."

Ned had promised he would eat all his food, and I was sure he did not want to break his promise on the first night I was with him.

"Ned, I think you had enough. You did very well. Good boy. Now how about we have ice cream?" Richard asked as he tousled Ned's hair.

"Oh yes! Thank you, Daddy," Ned answered, then, turning to me, he asked, "What kind of ice cream is your favorite, Trudy?"

"Chocolate, of course," I replied, giving him a big smile.

"Yes, that is my favorite too," he said.

As we ate our ice cream, I asked, "Ned, tomorrow night, how about if you and Roger help me make supper? Would you like that?"

Both boys nodded.

"What would we make?" Ned asked.

"What do you like to eat?"

"Chicken fingers," both boys replied together.

I smiled at them and said, "Chicken fingers it will be then."

Ned finished his ice cream, then said, "You know how to make chicken fingers? Are they hard to make? I always thought they were hard to make because the cook never makes them."

I just had to laugh. I found Ned to be a very charming, delightful little boy.

"Oh, I think they're easy to make. I'll show you both how to make them tomorrow night," I replied.

Richard left shortly after the supper dishes were cleared. I felt a little nervous to be alone with the boys for the first time. The boys showed me to the living room and asked to watch a show on TV. As I watched the show, I found it hard to keep my eyes open. I was very tired; the last two days had been such a whirlwind.

"What time do you boys go to bed?" I asked during a commercial break.

"We both go to bed at eight," Roger replied. "But Ned always keeps getting up and plays around."

"No, I won't," cried Ned. He looked at me and said, "I promised to be good. When you say it's time to go to bed, I will."

I looked at the time. We had another half hour to go, so I asked, "Do you have homework to do tonight? We should have done that before TV time."

"No, not tonight. But I could read my storybook to you, if you want," Roger replied.

"That would be lovely, Roger. Would you like that, Ned?" I said, not wanting Ned to feel left out.

"Ned can't sit still long enough; he always interrupts," Roger protested.

"I'll be good. I won't interrupt. I'll listen to the story," Ned said as he came to sit close to me.

Roger went to get his book, then came to sit on my other side. He opened the book at the bookmark and started to read. For a fourth-grader, he read very well. I was impressed.

When he stopped reading, I told the boys, "Roger, I like the way you read. And you, Ned, you sat and listened; you were so good."

It was a few minutes before eight, so I told the boys to go get ready for bed. I gave them a few minutes to get their pajamas on and brush their teeth, then I went up to tuck them in.

As I came into Ned's room, I saw both boys kneeling by the bed. They had their heads bowed and their eyes closed.

Ned said, "Thank you for sending Trudy to us. Take care of Daddy and Roger."

Then, Roger said, "Yes, Lord, thank You for Trudy. Please help Ned keep his promise."

Just as Roger finished, Ned opened his eyes and when he saw me, he quickly got into his bed.

Roger passed by me as he went to his room and said, "'Night, Trudy. See you in the morning."

"Good night, Roger, have a good sleep," I said, then went to tuck Ned in.

"Are you ready to go to sleep, Ned?" I asked, tucking his blankets tightly around him.

"Yes, but you have to read me a story, please," he said.

"Oh, I do, do I?" I said with a big smile on my face.

He handed me the open book he had been holding and said, "Can you read this story? It's about Jesus loving the little children."

I looked at the page. It had a picture of a man in a long robe, extending his hand to the little children, and the children were running toward him. I read the story to Ned, and as I did, I felt a strange comfort come over me.

"Did you like the story, Trudy? That's my favorite story; Jesus loves little children, even those who are not good. Did you know that, Trudy?" he said in a very serious way.

"Yes, Ned," I replied, but I wasn't at all certain I believed it.

I said good night to Ned and went to the living room to wait for Richard. I loved this room. It was very spacious, with a large brown leather sectional on one side and two overstuffed La-Z-Boy recliners on the other side, facing the fireplace and big-screen TV. Over the fireplace mantel was a large picture of a man trying to lasso a horse that was rearing up. On the back wall were a set of patio doors that led to a covered deck. I went to make myself comfortable in one of the recliners. As I sat, I felt that strange comfort again. I realized that I had not thought about Mom or John since I had gotten here. I felt hopeful and at peace with myself. Then, it occurred to me that what John had done was just what I needed. He had pushed me out for my own good. I remembered the note and regretted the words I had written and the mess that I had left.

I was watching the news when Richard walked in and asked, "How were the boys?"

"I think we had a good time, but I have to tell you something," I replied.

He gave me a strange look and said, "What did Ned do now?"

"Oh no, nothing like that. Ned was a super little boy. It's about me. Ned had me read his story about Jesus and the little children. He then asked me if I liked the story. I told him I did, but I think I should tell you that I don't believe in God. I have never needed religion in my life. I don't want to confuse Ned by telling him what I believe. Maybe I'm not the nanny Ned needs."

"Thank you for being honest with me. I should have asked you about your beliefs, but Ned was so insistent that I hire you that the subject never came up. I have a relationship with God and His Son Jesus. I don't consider it a religion; it's my way of living. Are you saying that you can't stay because of what we believe?"

"No, not at all. In fact, I'm willing to learn more. It's strange, but after I read the story, I felt comforted and at peace with my mother's death. It was a strange feeling," I replied.

Richard smiled and said, "Do you want to know what I think?" I nodded, so he continued, "I think Jesus is already working in your heart; He wants you to feel His love and peace."

Returning his smile, I said, "To be sure, I'll be asking you more about this in the future. Right now, though, I'm very tired. Would you have any sheets for the bed? I never unloaded my car, and my sheets are still somewhere in a box."

"I'm so sorry, I should have given you time to unpack your things. Please forgive me. Come right this way, and I'll show you where we keep those things," Richard said as he went out of the living room to a closet in the hall.

I followed him to the closet, where he handed me sheets, pillowcases, blankets, and some towels.

"If you need anything else, just help yourself."

"Thank you, Richard."

Richard helped me to the apartment door and once I was inside, he bid me goodnight and returned to the house.

As I made the bed, I realized how fast my life had changed; I now had a job and a new place to live. It made me smile just thinking about it. I got ready for bed then laid down. I felt so exhausted, the minute my head touched the pillow, I was asleep.

When I woke in the morning, I was a little disoriented. It took me a few seconds to remember where I was. I had slept so deeply; I don't think I moved once during the night. I had no idea when the family usually woke up, but I got up and took a shower.

I should have asked Richard when they usually get up, I thought.

I got dressed and decided to go to my car to get my things. As I walked up the driveway, I saw Tex on his way to the house.

As we passed each other, he said, "Good morning miss. Fine day we're having."

I gave him a smile. He tipped his cowboy hat and walked on.

I got my bags from my car and returned to the apartment. I was going to unpack, but then I thought, *If Tex is going to the house, he probably knows that Richard is already up. I'd better go see.*

When I got to the kitchen, the cook had already started breakfast. Richard and Tex were sitting at the table having coffee.

When Richard saw me, he said, "Good morning Trudy. How did you sleep?"

"I slept very well, thanks," I replied.

Richard stood up and said, "Come. I'll introduce you to Dell, our cook. She's Tex wife. You remember Tex from yesterday, right?"

I followed Richard into the kitchen where Dell was buttering toast. After Richard introduced us, she said, "It's nice to meet you, Trudy. Would you like some coffee?"

I accepted the coffee and returned to sit at the table with Richard and Tex.

"When do the boys get up, Richard?" I asked.

"They're usually up by eight," Richard answered, then returned to talk to Tex.

I then noticed Dell placing food containers in heating trays on the sideboard.

After she placed the last of the containers, she said, "Help yourselves; the food is ready."

Just as I was about to sit at the table with my plate of food, four ranch hands walked in. They went to get their food, then came to sit at the table.

When they were seated, Richard said, "Good morning, boys. I'd like to introduce you to Trudy, our new nanny." He then introduced me to each of them, explaining that they were temporary work hands.

I discovered that this was a working breakfast where ranch hands got their assignments for the day, so after I finished eating, I went to help Dell in the kitchen.

Breakfast was all finished when the boys walked in. Richard was the only one sitting at the table, working on his laptop. When Richard saw the boys, he closed the computer and greeted them.

After the boys had given their father a hug, Ned said, "Where is Trudy? Is she up yet?"

Before Richard could answer, Ned saw me and rushed over to hug me.

"Good morning, Ned. How did you sleep?" I asked, returning his hug.

Dell asked the boys what they wanted for breakfast but instead of answering Dell, Ned asked, "Trudy, would you make me breakfast?"

I looked at Dell; I did not want to overstep. I was unsure how she would feel about me making breakfast.

"What?! Don't you like my cooking, young man?" Dell said with a big smile on her face.

"I like your cooking. I just want Trudy to make my breakfast," Ned replied.

"Okay, Ned. What would you like for breakfast?" I asked.

"Pancakes with a lot of whipped cream and bananas on top. Roger likes that too. Don't you, Roger?" Ned said.

Roger nodded his head in agreement.

The pancake batter was already prepared, so all I had to do was grill the pancakes. I had the boys' breakfast made in no time.

Of course, Ned commented that they were the best pancakes he'd ever had.

When the boys finished eating, they returned their plates to the kitchen, then went to sit at the table with their dad.

I went to sit with them but realized that this was father-and-sons time, so I excused myself and went to the apartment. I unloaded the rest of my things from my car, as I would need it to take the boys to school. Richard had told me I could take the Jeep, but I felt more comfortable driving my own car. I was starting to unpack my things when there was a knock on the door.

When I opened it, there stood Ned.

Before I could say anything, he walked in and said, "We're already to go to school, Trudy."

"Okay, then. Let's go," I said.

He took my hand and we returned to the house to get Roger. When I told the boys, we were taking my car, Ned was delighted, but he told me he needed his car seat. They went to get the car seat then once we were all buckled in, we set off for school.

Ned was being his best little self, complimenting me on how nice my car was. Said he liked red cars. He talked for most of the way to school, telling me about the neighbors, including their names and what they farmed.

When I glanced in the rearview mirror, I saw Roger nodding to confirm Ned's pronouncements.

As we passed Liz's house, Ned said, "That's where Liz lives. She has three children, but I only play with Trevor."

"Why don't you play with the other two?" I asked, glancing up into the mirror again.

With a strange little look on his face, Ned answered, "Oh, they're just little, and they're girls. Trevor calls them the twins."

Suppressing a laugh, I said, "Oh, I see."

I'm going to enjoy taking care of these boys, I thought.

A few weeks later, my references checked out, and I passed my background check, so Richard officially hired me as the boys' nanny.

I now officially had a job and a place to call home.

As the days went by, I got to know the family's routine. I found that Richard had a varied work schedule, we never knew when he'd be home. The only time we knew he'd be home was on weekends.

One evening Richard returned home and found me watching a movie. He came in and sat on the La-Z-Boy next to me.

"How were the boys?" he asked.

"They were good, Richard," I said, then asked, "May I ask you a question?"

When he nodded, I asked, "What was Ned's mother's name?"

I think he was a little surprised by the question, but he answered it.

"Her name was Amanda," he said, then, to my surprise, he added, "She died when Ned was born."

"Did she die in childbirth?" I asked, imagining how awful that must have been.

"No, Amanda died in a car accident. The paramedics had to cut Ned out of her; otherwise, he would have died too," Richard informed me.

Seeing the deep hurt in his eyes, I said, "I'm so sorry, Richard. I shouldn't have asked."

"It's still very hard for me to talk about it; but I think you need to know what happened. Both boys don't know how their mother died. All they know is that she's now with Jesus," Richard replied in a sorrowful way.

"Who helped care for the boys?" I asked, hoping I wasn't being too nosy.

"My mother lived here and took care of the boys until three years ago. She suffered a heart attack; after that, she just wasn't the same. Sadly, she had to go into a nursing home. She died last spring. The boys are comforted to know that their mother and grandmother are together now; they're both with Jesus," Richard said.

"That is so sad. It must have been very hard on you," I said with sympathy.

"At first, it was unbearable. But over time, with the help of friends and neighbors, I found my way. My friend encouraged me to read the Bible and to pray for God's help. It took some time, but I'm at peace now," he answered.

When he said that, I became very uneasy. I had never considered praying for my mother, but I'm sure Mary had.

"Do you think that praying to God helped you?" I asked.

"Yes, I'm sure it did. After Amanda died, I was so angry. I could not make sense of what had happened to us. We were so happy. We loved Roger and looked forward to having a new baby. After her death, I was a mess and needed a lot of help. I went to grief counseling and met someone who helped me realize that I needed God in my life. He replaced the anger with His peace. I still miss Amanda and probably always will. But, you know, God cares, and He knows how much I can take. He knew we needed help, so that's why He sent you to us," Richard replied.

"Do you think it was God who brought me here?" I asked, adding, "How can that be? I never cared or thought about God. Can He work with someone who doesn't even know Him?"

"Oh yes. God's ways are not our ways," Richard replied. "I've got an early meeting in the morning. Good night, Trudy."

I said good night, but I stayed up for a while, thinking about what Richard had said.

Maybe it was God who had brought me here. Was that little light, that glimmer of hope, I saw from Him?

On Friday afternoons Richard usually had a barbecue for the people who worked on the ranch. It was a time to unwind and catch up on what had happened during the week. During my first barbecue, I got to know the people who worked on the ranch. I also learned more about Richard: he had a brother named Neil who had left the ranch shortly after Amanda's accident. Neil was now in the States, studying to be a veterinarian. The boys had spent the week regaling me with all the details of their family life, and I found it very odd that they had never mentioned having an uncle. I also learned that Richard had a lady friend and that they had once been engaged.

The barbecue lasted into the evening, and it was time for me to bring Ned inside and put him to bed. Ned had been on his best behavior the whole time, enjoying being with the ranch hands.

"Trudy, you're the best thing that ever happened to Ned," Tex told me, as the two of us observed Ned.

I was a little surprised by the comment, so I asked, "Why do you say that?"

"Well, tonight Ned has eaten all the food on his plate without once complaining or demanding Richard's attention. Ned usually has one or two temper tantrums, but not tonight. I can see Richard is relaxed, his old self again. And I know it's all your doing," Tex answered.

"Tex, was Ned really that bad?" I asked. I had not seen Ned misbehave once, despite what Richard and everyone else told me, I couldn't believe that he ever would. It couldn't all be my doing.

Tex smiled and said, "He was so good tonight. Thanks for all you're doing."

I didn't think I was doing anything special with Ned; I was taking care of him. Ned was a delightful little boy, and I loved the way he viewed his world. He loved learning new things and often asked me to show him how to do things I never would have thought of showing him. After the first supper the boys and I cooked together, Ned asked me if I would show him how to bake his favorite cookies: double chocolate, chocolate-chip cookies. We asked Dell for the recipe, and when she gave us the recipe book, Ned looked through it and asked if we could make every recipe in the book.

As time went on, Saturday mornings became the time for us to bake. Roger had no interest in baking, so he spent time with his father. Baking time was a special time for Ned and me. Although Saturday was my day off, I enjoyed Ned's and my time together, and it quickly became my favorite time to be with him.

5

As the months passed, Ned became more and more emotionally attached to me.

One night, while I was reading him a story, Ned asked, "Trudy, can I call you Mom? I want you to be my mother. Please, Trudy, say yes! Please, please!"

Surprised and speechless, I just looked at him. His green eyes were focused on me, entreating me to say yes.

"Ned, that's very nice of you to say, but I couldn't possibly be your mother. I'm your nanny. You'll have to talk to your father about this," I said, firmly but gently, so as not to hurt his feelings.

Ned would not be put off.

"Trudy you do everything a mother does," Ned persisted. "You take care of me, you wash my clothes, you cook my food, you take me to school, you tuck me in at night, and you read me stories. You do everything Liz does for her kids. Why can't I call you Mom?"

I didn't reply. Ned was about to cry, so I put my hand on his head and rubbed his hair. After a moment, I said, "Ned, you'll have to talk to your father about this. Now, young man, it's time you went to sleep."

"Okay. I will ask him in the morning. Good night, Trudy. I love you," he said.

Ned turned on his side and fell asleep.

I sat there looking at him. This was the first time Ned said that he loved me.

As I made my way downstairs, I thought, *What in the world am I to do now? I can't be Ned's mom, but how can I keep saying no to him without breaking his heart?*

When I went into the kitchen the next morning, Ned and Richard were sitting at the table.

When I saw Ned, I said, "You're up early."

Richard looked at me and said, "He was at my bedroom door, waiting for me to get up. The first thing he asked me was if he could call you Mom." Then, he looked at Ned and said, "Trudy is a lady I hired to take care of you. She's your nanny. When you're older, you won't need a nanny, and then Trudy will go care for someone else. She can't be your mom."

When Ned heard what his father said, he cried, "No! Trudy will never go away! I want her to be my mother. I never had a mother before. Oh, please say that Trudy can be my mom!"

Ned started to cry. Big tears rolled down his face, and through his tears, he sobbed, "Please, Daddy, ask Trudy to be my mom. I love her just like I would if she were my mom. Jesus sent her to me, Daddy. I just know it."

Richard turned in his seat, picked up Ned, and sat him on his lap. I could tell that Richard was having a hard time deciding what to say.

"Ned, we never asked Trudy what she thinks about being your mom," Richard said.

They both looked at me, and Ned said, "Trudy, would you be my mom?"

Now I was the one who did not know what to say. I did not want to hurt Ned, so I said, "Ned, how about if you call me Mom at home. When we go to school or into town, you can call me Trudy. Will that be okay? Is that all right with you, Richard?"

I looked at the two of them and thought, *Oh Ned, I feel the same way you do. I don't want to ever leave you.*

"It's okay for now," Ned conceded.

Richard nodded and said, "Ned, this is very important. Trudy and I must talk about this. For now, you can call her Mom at home but nowhere else. Is that understood?"

"Oh yes! I will keep it a secret until you tell me I can tell everyone," Ned replied, then looked at me and said, "Okay, Mom?"

When I returned from dropping the boys off at school, I was surprised to see Richard was still at home.

The minute I stepped inside the house, he said, "We have to talk."

The way he said it, I thought for sure I was in trouble, but as I sat at the table, he said, "Trudy, I'm sorry to place you in this predicament. I should have known Ned would come up with this solution to his problem. He's always said he wanted a mom. I just never thought he would be the one to pick who his mother was going to be." I didn't say anything, so he continued, "I don't know if you know this, but I was engaged, and we were going to be married; the wedding was all planned. But Ned put up such a big fuss that we called it off. Star said that Ned had to come first."

"Star was your fiancée? Are you still seeing each other?" I asked.

"Yes, but Ned doesn't know. Neither does Roger. Star and I are still engaged and plan to get married, but we're waiting for Ned to get a little older. Star is a school principal and expert on child behavior. She knows Ned's history and does not want to add to his trauma. She says that Ned is afraid of losing me. He lost his mother, then his grandmother. He loved his grandmother; she was the one who took care of him from the start. When she fell ill and could not take care of him any longer, he became a very naughty boy. Now that you're here, Ned is so different. He's a nice little boy again, much more pleasant to be with," Richard said.

"When I first came here a few months ago, I never dreamed I'd be a nanny to such a wonderful little boy. I love taking care of both boys, especially Ned, but I know I could never be his mother. When he called me Mom, it felt a little strange. When you marry Star, she'll be his mother," I said.

"Unfortunately, I know for certain he'll never accept Star as his mom. When Ned gets an idea, he doesn't stop until he gets what he wants. He's not going to be satisfied with just calling you Mom. He wants you to be his mother, and he wants the entire world to know that you are," Richard said.

"So, what are you going to do?" I asked.

"I think we should let Ned take the next step and see what he comes up with," he replied.

"Okay, I'm willing to go along with that," I said, but I had some misgivings.

What if I don't get along with Star? This could get very complicated! Ned, what are you asking of me?

In the coming weeks, Ned called me Mom at home and talked Roger into doing the same.

We were having supper one evening when Richard told the boys he was going to take them to the big city that weekend.

"Will Mom be coming too?" Ned asked.

Richard looked at me and said, "Trudy can come too, if she wants. You'll have to ask her."

Ned was so happy. He looked at me and said, "Are you going to come, Mom? It's going to be a lot of fun. Please say you will."

"Oh, I don't know, Ned. Maybe your father wants to make this trip with just the two of you," I said, looking to see what Richard's reaction would be.

But Ned would not take no for an answer. "Dad said you could come. Please, Mom, come with us."

"Okay, I'll come. I haven't been to the big city in a long time," I answered.

Ned was so delighted, he jumped off his chair and came to hug me.

Early Saturday morning we set off for the city. Ned and I sat in the backseat, while Roger sat in the front passenger seat.

Ned was very talkative. "Mom, did you bring your swimsuit? We'll go on the waterslide. I can go all by myself on the little one. Right, Dad?"

Ned waited for his father to respond before he continued.

Richard said, "Yes, Ned, you can."

Ned quickly changed the subject, saying, "Mom, did you know that Roger will be getting a horse when he turns ten? I'll get one too when I turn ten. Right, Dad?"

Again, Ned waited for his father to respond.

"Yes, Ned, you will," Richard said.

This continued for most of the ride, making it very entertaining.

After we checked into our hotel rooms, Richard said he had a meeting and would join us later. The boys and I changed into our swimsuits and headed for the water park. Once at the water park, Roger asked if he could go to the wave pool, so I let him go. Ned wanted to go down the waterslide, so I let him lead me to it. When it was our turn to go on, the lifeguard told us that Ned was too short to go down the slide by himself; I would have to accompany him. This pleased Ned all the more. I had never gone down a big slide like this one and was a little apprehensive. What if I lost control of Ned? But the ride down was fun, and when we splashed into the pool below, I was able to hold on to Ned. We must have gone up those stairs and down the slide ten times. Ned was like a little Energizer battery—he wanted to keep going—but I was tired.

"Ned let's go find Roger. I wonder how he's doing," I said.

Ned was only too happy to obey.

At first, we did not see Roger, and I became concerned.

Just as I spotted him, Ned said, "There he is, Mom. I see him; he's over on the other side." He looked at me and whispered, "Whoops, I called you Mom. Sorry."

Smiling, I tousled his hair.

We sat on the lounge chairs and watched Roger on his wakeboard. He was very good at standing on the board. When he spotted us, he made his way toward us. As he toweled off, he said, "Thank you for letting me do this, Trudy. Dad has never let me go in the wave pool."

Before I could answer Roger, I received a call from Richard. After the call, I said, "We'd better be going, boys. Your dad said he will meet us at the restaurant in half an hour. Let's go back to the room and change."

We were just about to enter the restaurant when Ned stopped and said, "What is *she* doing with dad?"

I looked in the direction Ned was looking and saw Richard with a beautiful dark-haired lady.

So that was Richard's lady friend? Why hadn't he told me we were going to meet with her? I wondered.

"Dad's with Star! I didn't know they were back together," Roger said in surprise.

Roger and I started to walk again, but Ned would not budge, so I said, "Roger, you go on. I think I need to have a little talk with Ned."

I took Ned and went to sit on a bench just outside the restaurant.

"Ned, why don't you want to meet Star?" I asked. He was looking down and did not answer me, so I asked again, "Ned, what's the matter? Come on, talk to me."

"Trudy, if Star marries Dad, you will never be my mother. I don't want Star to be my mother; I want you," he answered in the most sorrowful tone.

"Oh! Did you think that your dad and I would get married?" I asked.

He nodded.

I smiled and said, "Ned, it doesn't work that way. Your father loves Star; he doesn't love me."

"But he could, if Star wasn't around," he replied.

I did not know how to answer him without hurting his feelings, so I just said, "If they married, I would still be your nanny. Now, please, Ned. You have to let your dad be with the lady he loves. What if your dad sent me away?"

"No! He wouldn't!" Ned cried.

"Well, Ned, you're asking your dad to send the lady he loves away. Is that fair?" I asked.

I saw Ned's attitude change. He looked at me and said, "Okay, Mom, let's go in the restaurant."

Ned walked in with his head held high.

When we were seated, Richard asked, "Is everything all right?"

I looked at Ned and answered, "Yes, I think so."

"Good, because I already ordered for you. Ned, I ordered spaghetti with those little meatballs you like so much. Trudy, I hope you like that too because I ordered a plate for you as well," Richard said.

"I'm sure I'll love it, Richard, thank you." I replied.

Richard smiled and said, "Trudy, I'd like to introduce you to Star, my fiancée."

Star extended her hand and said, "Trudy, it's very nice to meet you. Richard has told me about you. I'm very happy you have come to help Richard out."

I shook her hand and said, "I'm pleased to meet you too, Star."

Throughout the exchange of greetings, Ned just looked straight ahead, not saying anything, which was not at all like the boy I knew.

I instantly liked Star. She was very friendly and easy to talk to.

We had just finished eating when Roger said, "Trudy let me go to the wave pool. It was so much fun. Dad, I can stand up on the board and ride the wave for a long time."

Richard looked at me and said, "I'm surprised they let you in. Aren't you supposed to be twelve before you can go in there?"

"Well, they let me in, no one asked me any questions," Roger replied.

Richard looked at me again but did not say anything.

The look made me feel very uneasy, and I thought, *I didn't know. Roger never told me that you hadn't let him go in the wave pool before.*

Shortly after our time in the city, winter descended upon us. I liked the way it transformed the ranch. Snow had fallen, and everything was covered in a blanket of white. I was waiting in the library for the boys to come out of school when I heard, "Is that you, Trudy? What are you doing here?"

I turned and saw Al, a guy I had met when I took a computer course, in college.

"Al? Hi! I could ask you the same," I replied, surprised to see him there.

But, before he could ask me about my life, I asked, "What are you doing in this little place? I thought you were going to make it big in computers."

"Sometimes things don't turn out like you want," he said and then asked, "Would you like to go for coffee?"

I looked at my watch and said, "I'm afraid I don't have much time. Just a quick one."

On the museum side, there was a small area where patrons could go sit and have coffee. We got our coffees, then went to sit at a table.

"So, what are you doing here, Al?" I asked.

He took a sip of coffee and said, "Oh, I'm a sales rep. And what do you do?"

"I'm a nanny. I take care of two wonderful boys," I replied, hoping I hadn't said too much.

I kept asking Al questions so he would not have a chance to ask me any. When I finished my coffee, I stood up and said goodbye.

During the next week I kept running into Al. Finally, he asked if he could come see me.

"I don't know about that. I'm not sure the boys' father would like it if I brought someone home," I replied.

"What? You can't have any visitors? What kind of a place do you live in? You're not in a cult, are you?" he asked.

I did not like his pushy manner or the way he spoke, so, instead of answering him, I said, "I've got to go. Goodbye, Al."

With that, I got up and left.

That evening Tex called the house to say that there was an Al who wanted to see me. Without asking me, Richard told Tex to bring him to the house. As I waited for Al, I felt a little panicked and thought, *I've never told him where I lived. How did he find out? What will Richard think of this?*

When we heard the knock on the door, Richard was the one to open the door and met Al.

"Is Trudy here? I've got something I want to give her," he said, pushing himself through the doorway.

I was standing beside Richard when I saw Al, I asked, "Al, what are you doing here? Why would you want to give me anything? I don't even know you that well."

He gave me an obstinate look and said, "Trudy, would you care for my bear until I get my own place? I live in a small boarding room and have no place for it."

He handed me the bear before I could even say a word. I wasn't prepared for how heavy the bear was, so when he let go of it, it just fell to the floor with a strange thud.

"That's a heavy bear," I commented.

Al gave me another strange look and said, "Yeah, it has sand at the bottom to make it stand." Then, he nodded at me and said, "Thanks, Trudy, for your help. I'll come back to get it after Christmas."

Al turned around and walked away.

As Richard closed the door, he asked, "What a strange guy. How well do you know this fellow?"

I was so embarrassed, I'm sure my face was bright red. It took me a few seconds to answer. Finally, I said, "I met him at school a long time ago. He's been hanging out at the library this past week. I don't know how he knew I was here; I never told him where I lived. Oh, what am I going to do with this thing now?"

"You know, the police are having a fund-raiser for the kids' hospital. They're gathering teddy bears and putting them in jail. If you want your bear back, you have to make a donation to pay its bail. We could put the bear in jail for the holidays, and when Al returns for it, he'll have to pay the bail," Richard suggested.

"Oh, that's a good idea, Dad," Ned said. "Don't you think so, Mom?"

After I agreed that it was, Richard said, "Okay, I'll take the bear to the police station on my way to work tomorrow morning."

The next day, as I returned from bringing the boys to school, I saw a police car drive up to the house, with Richard right behind it. When Richard told me the police wanted to speak to me, I became very uneasy. Richard then told me what had happened when he got to the station: a police dog sniffed out dope in the bear, and when they opened up the bear, they found a stash of drugs.

We all went to sit at the table, then the police chief asked, "Do you know where this Al lives?"

When I told him no, he looked at me as if he did not believe me.

"Trudy, did you know what was in the bear?" When I said no, he continued, "Trudy, why would anyone leave this stuff with someone he barely knows?"

"I don't know anything about this Al. We met years ago in school. I hadn't seen him until last Wednesday. He's the one who pushed the bear on me; I didn't want anything to do with it. If I knew there was dope in it, do you think I would have let Richard bring it to you?" I said in a breaking voice.

Richard saw how upset I was getting, so he said, "Chief, we both know Trudy had nothing to do with this. If Trudy knew anything, I know she would tell us."

"Yeah, okay. I've got a job to do. Now, when this guy comes for his bear, please let us know," the chief said. "I'll see myself out."

Christmas was just a few weeks away, and with the way the Lance family celebrated the holidays, I all but forgot about Al. With the boys' help, Richard strung lights up on all the pine trees surrounding the house. They even strung lights around the entire perimeter of the house, making the place look magical.

I had never seen Ned so happy.

Then, out of the blue, as we were having supper one night, Ned said to his father, "You know, I have a friend at school who said his mom and dad adopted him. Could Trudy adopt me and be my real mother? Then, I could call her Mom all the time and tell everyone that she's my mom."

I sat there in amazement and thought, *Oh, you clever little boy! So that's what you came up with.*

I looked at Richard and saw he was as stunned as I was by the question.

"Do you know what *adopt* means Ned?" Richard asked.

"Yes, Dad, I know. My friend said that he did not have a mom and dad until they adopted him. If Trudy adopted me, then I'd have a mom," Ned replied with the biggest grin on his face.

"But, Ned, do you know what you're asking Trudy to do? It's a big step; it would change her entire life. It would mean Trudy would be responsible for you all the time, even on her days off. We'll have to discuss this and see what we can do," Richard replied.

I knew Ned would not let this idea go and was thankful for how Richard had answered him.

During the next week Ned asked us every day if we had decided about the adoption.

Then, one night as I was helping him into bed, Ned asked, "Trudy, don't you want to adopt me? Why is it taking so long for you to decide?"

"Ned, that is a very important matter; we don't want to rush in making this decision. You have a daddy. Nannies don't usually adopt the kids they care for. You are Richard's little boy, and he is the only one who can say what happens to you," I replied.

"But you would adopt me if Dad said you could, wouldn't you?"

I could see that Ned was close to tears. I hugged him and said, "We'll have to wait until your dad and I talk some more. Now, Ned, please go to sleep."

Once I knew Ned was asleep, I went to find Richard. I knocked on the door to his office, something I very rarely did, and asked to speak to him.

"Trudy, is something wrong? Is Ned sick?" Richard asked, surprised to see me at his office door.

"No Richard, Ned is all right physically. He asked me why I did not want to adopt him. He was very upset. I don't think he will ever stop asking. Is there something you can do?" I asked.

"Oh, that again. You're right: he's not going to drop it. Trudy, I never asked you this, but do you want to be Ned's mother?" Richard said.

Before I could answer, I thought, *Oh boy,* that *is a loaded question. How can I answer that?*

I looked at Richard and said, "Well, I do love that little boy. I've been thinking about this since the day he first asked me if he could call me Mom. It's such a big decision to make. So many questions have not been answered. It could complicate things between you and Star, or Star and me. Oh, I just don't know. Richard, would you let me be Ned's mother?"

"Trudy, I've also been thinking. And if it's going to make Ned happy, that's what I'm willing to do. If you agree to be Ned's mother, I'll take care of all the details. Don't worry about causing conflicts; you've answered our prayers. Now what do you say?" Richard asked.

"Really? You would let me adopt your son? Yes, Richard, I'm willing. I can't see not having Ned with me," I answered.

"Okay, then, I think we have the answer for Ned, but let's wait until he asks again before we tell him. I'll start asking about how we would do this," Richard replied.

A few days before Christmas, with the boys out of school for the Christmas holidays, Ned brought up the subject again.

Richard told him about our decision, then said, "Ned, there's a lot to think about before we determine if we are going to do this. I must get some advice from someone who knows about adoptions. I don't even know who that could be. Let me see what I can find out. We will talk more then. Okay, Ned?"

Ned nodded his head and said, "But don't take too long."

Richard smiled and said, "Star wants me to go to a Christmas party tonight. There might be someone there who would know about how adoptions are done. I'll find out. Ned, please be a good boy for Trudy, and I'll see you tomorrow morning."

The next day, as we were having breakfast, Richard said, "I found a lawyer who specializes in adoptions. I have an appointment with him this afternoon."

I saw Ned's eyes grow bigger as he realized what Richard was saying. "Oh, Daddy, thank you."

"Ned, I'm just going to talk to him; it doesn't mean we can do this yet. Now, don't get ahead of yourself. We'll have to wait and see what the lawyer says," Richard said.

"Yes, Daddy," Ned replied.

A short time after Richard left, Ned came to ask me, "Mom, how long will it take for Dad to come home?"

"I don't know, Ned. Just be patient," I replied but I didn't tell him I was as anxious as he was.

Ned kept asking when his father would be returning. Every time he asked, I would tell him to be patient. This went on until his father came home.

Finally, Ned saw Richard's Jeep drive up to the house. Ned ran outside and went to meet his dad. I could see him jumping up and down and heard him ask, "Dad, what did the man say? What did he say?"

Richard picked him up, and as they entered the house, Richard said, "Ned, relax. You are getting too excited. Let me take off my coat, then we'll all sit down and talk about it."

Once everyone was seated, Richard said, "Okay, Ned, the lawyer said that it can be done, but it might take time. We'll have to meet with a family judge. He's the one who will decide how things are going to be done. He said that we would all have to talk to the judge, Ned—you and me, Roger, Trudy, and Star. He has to know how everyone feels about the adoption."

When Ned heard Star's name, I saw his face fall, his expression changing from joy to sadness.

He asked, "Why does Star have to talk to the judge?"

"Ned, you know that Star is very special to me. I want her to be my wife. When we marry, she will be your stepmother."

This made Ned even more upset. I knew how he felt about Star and was about to intervene but before I could say anything, he cried, "Dad, I don't want Star to be my mother! I want Trudy."

I went to sit beside him and put my arm around his shoulders. "Ned, my dear sweet boy, please don't be upset. You should be happy that your father has a special lady. She makes him very happy. I know that your dad wants you to be happy. He went to see the lawyer so that I can become your mother. You can have a mother and a stepmother," I said, wiping his teary face.

"I can?" Ned replied.

Richard smiled and said, "Yes, that's right. This is our family, and we can make it like we want."

When Ned smiled, I saw the relief in his face.

Richard continued, "There's one more thing. I have invited Star to come for Christmas. She doesn't have to be anyone's mom. She's my friend. Ned, can I ask you to please be nice to her?"

Ned looked at me and said, "Yes, Daddy. I will be nice to Star. Trudy is special to me, and I know that Star is special to you."

That night, when I went to tuck Ned into bed, I noticed that he was a little quiet, so I asked, "Is something the matter? Did the talk we had upset you?"

"No, it's not that," Ned replied in a soft voice.

"Okay, little man, I know you, and you're not really yourself right now. Let's have it; tell me what's wrong," I said.

After a few seconds, Ned said, "Dad has been seeing her, but he never brings her here. I guess Star must not like me very much. I was kind of mean to her. I guess I should say I'm sorry. Do you think she hates me?"

"No, I don't think she hates you. She knows kids and can tell when they're acting up. If you tell her you're sorry, I'm sure she will forgive you. Now, have you said your prayers?" I said.

Ned went to kneel at his bedside and said, "Jesus, thank you for

Trudy, and please forgive me for being mean to Star. Please take care of Dad and Roger." He hesitated a second and then added, "And Star."

Christmas was fast approaching. It was a Lance family tradition to go into the woods to find the special tree that would become their Christmas tree. We took the snowmobiles and headed out, with Richard and Roger on one snowmobile, and Ned and me on the other. I had never been on a snowmobile, so Richard gave me a quick lesson on how to operate it. Richard went first, and I followed in his track. After a few minutes, I found that this was a lot of fun. It did not take long to find a tree, as there were so many to choose from. Ned picked the tree he thought was the best, so Richard chopped it down.

"It's too bad we had to cut the tree. It's so beautiful," I commented.

"Oh, don't feel bad; all the trees in this area are going to be pushed down. We need more land to graze the horses. A ranch can't be all in trees. But you're right about seeing such a beautiful tree cut down. It is for Christmas, though, so we'll get to enjoy seeing it all decorated," Richard said.

Once we had the tree at the house, it was another thing to get it *into* the house, for it was so big. After cutting off some branches and pushing and pulling, we finally had it standing in the traditional place in the living room, then we all stood back and admired it. It took up an entire corner of the room and reached to the top of the nine-foot ceiling.

"I don't think we'll have enough decorations to trim this tree. It looks a lot bigger in the house. I'll call Star to ask her to stop at the store and bring us some," Richard said.

When Richard went to make the call, Ned came to me and asked, "Is Star coming tonight?"

"I suppose so. It will be fun having her help us, don't you think?" I asked.

Richard returned from making the call and said, "Star has

decorations, she's going to bring them. Now let's go get the ones we have."

We all went downstairs, then returned each carrying a box of decorations to the tree. Richard and Roger strung the lights. As soon as they were on, Ned and I put on the garland. Most of the decorations were on the tree when Star arrived at the house. Richard went to greet her with a kiss, then took the two boxes of decorations from her and brought them close to the tree. Once we had all the decorations on the tree and it was lit, the tree looked spectacular. Roger helped Richard place the big gold star on the top, and it was all done.

"Well, that calls for some hot chocolate," Richard said. "Come, Star, I like the way you make it."

As they left the room, Ned went to sit on one of the La-Z-Boys. He had been very quiet ever since Star arrived.

I went over to see what was troubling him, and he told me, "Trudy, remember last night when I said I'd tell Star I was sorry? I don't know if I can."

I took his hand and said, "Oh, I see. Well, if you truly are sorry, you need to do it, Ned. Remember, Star loves your dad, and I'm sure she loves you too. This is something you have to do on your own."

He nodded his head and said, "Okay, Mom, I know. But will you be there when I do it?"

When Richard and Star returned with the steaming cups of hot chocolate, we all sat on the floor in front of the tree. With Christmas music playing in the background, we sipped our drinks and sang along with the music. It was then I realized how much I had missed during my growing-up years. My family had never done anything like this.

After Ned finished his drink, he went to Richard and said, "Dad, can I talk to you alone?"

"Sure, Ned. Let's go to my study," Richard replied.

As they walked toward the archway leading into the living room, Ned turned to me and asked, "Mom, can you come with us?"

When we got to Richard's study, Ned went to sit on Richard's lap. I could tell he was struggling with what he had to do.

"Well, Ned, what's up?" Richard asked.

"Dad, I have to say I'm sorry to Star for being mean to her. I *am* sorry, but I don't know if I can say that to her. What will she think?" Ned replied.

"Is that what you've been fretting about? Ned, Star loves you, and if you tell her you're sorry, she'll forgive you. Don't be afraid of doing the right thing," Richard advised.

"Okay, Dad. I'll do it," Ned said, nodding his head.

When we returned to the living room, Ned walked straight to Star and said, "Miss Star, can I talk to you?"

"Why, yes, Ned. What is it?" Star said as she looked at Richard.

Richard just shrugged and went to sit by Roger.

"Miss Star, I want to say I'm sorry for being mean to you. Please forgive me," Ned said, looking down.

Star reached out to him, lifted his chin, looked into his eyes, and said, "Of course I forgive you, Ned. You are very special to me; please forgive me for causing you any pain."

She then hugged Ned. To everyone's surprise, Ned returned the hug. I could see that both had tears rolling down their cheeks.

Then, wiping away her tears, Star said, "Now, this is the best Christmas present I have ever gotten."

6

Later, as I was returning from putting Ned to bed, Star called out from the living room, "Trudy, come sit with me. I'd like to get to know you better."

I went in and sat beside her on the couch.

"What brought you to us?" she asked.

"Well, I don't really know. Ned believes that Jesus brought me here," I replied.

"Is there something that made you leave home?" Star asked.

"Yes, you could say that. My stepfather threw me out. After my mother died, I went into a deep depression. I felt like I did not have anything to live for; I was so lost. You see, I had been my mother's caregiver. When she passed, my life went with her." I went on to tell Star what John had done and how I had come to be here.

"I'm sorry to hear your mother passed. It must have been hard on you," Star replied, then asked, "How are you now? You don't seem depressed."

"It's very strange. As I drove here, the depression left, and a calm came over me. When I saw the ad in the paper, I knew I had to come. I felt like a load was taken off my shoulders," I replied.

"May I ask about your mother? What did she do?" Star asked.

I was a little surprised by the question. I had hardly ever spoken of my mother since her death and didn't want to break down in tears in front of Star.

"My mom was a seamstress. She had a business designing and

sewing formal gowns; you know, for grads and weddings and such," I told Star, glad that I could say that much without tearing up.

"What was her name?" Star asked.

"Her name was Ellen," I said.

Then, to my surprise, Star gasped and said, "Was she Dresses by Ellen?"

When I nodded, Star continued, "I knew her. I met her once at a luncheon the grad mothers were giving. This summer we heard of her passing. It upset the girls at school, especially this year's grads. She definitely made beautiful gowns."

"Oh my goodness! You knew my mother? It's so nice to hear your kind words about her. I loved the dresses she made. She took care to make every dress the way each girl wanted it to be. She never let a dress out of her shop until she thought it was perfect."

As I remembered those days, big tears started to form in my eyes and roll down my cheeks.

"It's okay, Trudy, you don't have to talk about it anymore," Star said.

"No, it's all right. It's the first time that I've really spoken of my mom since she passed. It's nice to remember her," I said.

Star smiled and handed me a tissue.

"It must be hard to spend Christmas without your mother," Star said.

"No, not really. We never celebrated Christmas. We never had lights or exchanged gifts. My stepfather, John, did not believe in God and said people who did were just mental. In his house only his opinion mattered. He was a good dad, but I could not question what he believed," I said.

When Richard and Star heard that, they both sat up.

"You grew up never being told about God?" Star asked.

"Oh, I would hear things on TV and read things at the library, but I never asked John or Mom about it. One Christmas, I must have been ten, I asked John why we never got a Christmas tree. He looked at me and asked if I had gone mental. He made it sound like it was the worst thing one could become, so after that, I never asked again," I replied.

"Do you believe in God?" Star asked.

"Yes, I believe in God now. Growing up, though, it was something that was never discussed. The kids I went with never talked about it. But when I started reading Ned's Bible stories, I began to think I was missing something very special. Ned said that he had given his heart to Jesus. He has such a strong belief in Him. I wish I would have had that kind of belief when I was little," I said.

"Thanks for sharing that with us, Trudy," Richard said, then added, "I want to thank you for making it possible for Star to spend Christmas with all of us. We haven't been able to be together like this for a long time. In the past, Ned used to want all my attention and would not let Star close to me. He would constantly interrupt our conversations. The last time Star was here, Ned was playing with his Legos. He asked me to help him with what he was building. I was in the middle of something, so Star asked if she could help him. He got so upset, he picked up the Lego thing he was working on and threw it at Star, telling her that he did not want her help and asked her why she would not leave his dad alone."

"That's when we knew that getting married was not going to work. We postponed our wedding, and I stopped coming to the house. I could not cause Ned any more pain. Richard and I continued to see each other but spending time as a family was not possible. But ever since you got here, Ned has been a totally different little boy, and I thank you for that," Star said.

The next day was Christmas Eve. Ned was so excited. Tonight, there was going to be a special program at the church he went to. Ned had made a big production about inviting me, and I could not turn him down. He had asked me many times to come to church with him, but I always said I couldn't. The last time I had set foot in a church was when I was very young. I was very nervous about going, I didn't even know what to wear to church.

So I went to find Star and asked, "What are you going to wear for the program at church?"

"Oh, I was thinking I'd wear my dress pants and a blue sweater. And you, what will you wear?" she said.

I smiled and said, "Oh, Star, I don't know. I'm so nervous about going. Why am I feeling like this?"

"Trudy, just relax. Think of it like you're going to visit a friend. Wear something nice but comfortable. Stop worrying about it, and just go and enjoy the program. Come. Let's go have tea."

She gave me a little pat on the arm and went to make some tea.

When we got to the church later that evening, I was surprised to see so many people there. Everyone we met seemed very happy to see us. They greeted us with handshakes and hugs. I was introduced as the boys' nanny, and warmly welcomed.

After everyone had found a place to sit, the program started. We were all asked to join in to sing the first song: "Silent Night." It surprised me that they would sing a song I knew. Everyone there sang; it sounded so lovely.

The children's presentation was the Christmas story of Joseph and Mary. Ned was Joseph. I truly enjoyed it; I thought the kids all did their part perfectly.

When the presentation was over, the preacher started his talk. He spoke of God giving us a gift—the gift of eternal life. He spoke of God's love for the world, proved by sending His Only Son to die for our sins. Jesus gave up His life on a cross to give us that gift. It cost Jesus everything. Then, the preacher asked if anyone would like to accept that gift and become a child of God. I just about stood up and went forward. But there was so much I needed to know, I stayed in my chair. I decided that I would ask Richard, then I'd make my decision. Now I knew what church was about: learning how to live!

On Christmas morning I heard a knock at my door. When I went to the door, I found Ned standing in pajamas, with his boots on.

"Ned, what are you doing? Come in here before you freeze to

death. It's still dark and very cold out! Why didn't you put on your coat?" I said.

As I pulled him inside the apartment, he gave me a hug.

"Merry Christmas, Mom. I tried to wake up Dad and Roger, but they told me to go back to bed. I want everybody to get up, so we can open the presents."

I looked at the time and saw it was only seven.

I smiled and said, "Merry Christmas, Ned. You're up early. I'll get dressed and meet you in the house. You go now and get back in the house. Be quick, or you'll catch a cold."

When I got to the house, I found Ned sitting all alone at the table.

"Ned, why don't we have breakfast before the others get up? It'll just be me and you," I said.

Ned's face beamed with happiness. Other than our baking time on Saturdays, we didn't often have time alone together, with just the two of us.

"Okay, Mom. I'll just have Cheerios; I don't want to make you work on Christmas Day," he said.

I smiled at him, got two bowls out, and poured in the Cheerios. Ned went to get the milk, then we both went to sit at the table to eat.

As we ate, Ned asked, "Did you get a lot of presents when you were a little girl?"

I stirred the Cheerios in the milk a while and considered if I should tell him about my childhood.

"My family did not believe in Christmas. We did not exchange gifts, but sometimes when John wasn't at home, my mom would give me a present. But that didn't happen very often," I replied.

"Oh. Did you have a tree?" he asked.

"No, we did not. John said it was silly to put a tree in the house," I told him.

He looked at me and said. "Well, I don't think I would have liked that. Who is John? He sounds like the Grinch."

I had to laugh.

"John is my stepfather," I said. "He was nice, but he never believed in God, so he never celebrated Christmas."

As I finished speaking, Roger walked into the dining room, greeting me with "Merry Christmas, Trudy. Did Ned wake you up too?"

A short time later, Richard and Star walked in. When the boys saw their dad, they ran to him and greeted him with a Christmas hug. After giving Roger a hug, Richard picked Ned up and gave him a big bear hug, making Ned laugh with glee.

After Richard put Ned down, Ned went to Star and said, "Merry Christmas, Miss Star."

To everyone's astonishment, he then reached up to give her a kiss on the cheek and a little hug.

"I think Ned has waited long enough. Come on. Let's go open the presents," Richard said.

When I got to the living room, I was amazed to see all the presents under the tree. As a little girl, I had wished I could have had Christmas like this. Although Mom sometimes gave me a small gift if John was away, I had never thought of giving her one. At that thought, I felt like I was going to cry. I put on a big smile, though, and opened the present Richard and Star had given me. It was a Bible. Seeing it, the tears just flowed out. It was like they were washing away all the bad memories. I took the Bible and lifted it over my face to try to hide my tears. I didn't want to ruin anyone's Christmas.

Just as I was wiping away the last of the tears, Ned came to sit beside me and said, "Mom, this is from me. I hope you like it."

I took the little present he handed me. When I saw the little gift was wonderfully wrapped, I asked, "Did you wrap this all by yourself?"

"Yes, I did, Mom. I tried not to use too much tape. It makes it so hard to open," he replied.

"Okay, Ned, let's see what you got me," I said.

I carefully unwrapped the present to reveal a little jewelry box.

When I opened the box, I found a heart-shaped cameo brooch with antique brass braided around the outside. The cameo depicted a mother holding her child.

"Oh, this is beautiful, Ned! Thank you," I said, reaching over to give him a big hug.

"I'm so glad you like it, Mom," Ned said as he returned my hug. He then added, "I found it in the antique store Dad took me to. Dad said it's an heirloom. I don't know what an heirloom is, but I think it's pretty old. I can't wait till you are my real mom."

I smiled at him, took the brooch out of the little box, and pinned the cameo to the sweater I was wearing.

"You haven't opened the present I got you," I said.

"Is it that big one behind the tree?" When I nodded, he turned to his dad and said, "Dad, would you help me get my last present? I don't want to push the tree down."

Richard reached in and brought out the present, handing it to Ned.

When Ned unwrapped the gift, he exclaimed, "It's a SuperSlider! Thanks, Mom. Roger has one of these, and he can go really fast. Now I can race you, Roger." Turning to Richard, Ned asked, "Dad, do you think we could go sledding? I want to see how fast this sled goes."

"That's a good idea, Ned, but first we should go have breakfast," Richard replied.

We left the mess of wrapping paper on the living room floor and headed to the dining room.

Star took charge, saying, "Okay, boys, set the table. The food should be all warmed up by now. I hope you guys like quiche. Trudy, I think we should have some toast."

As I buttered the toast, I asked in a low voice, "Star, what is quiche?"

Star laughed out loud and said, "I think the boys are asking the same question."

Once everything was on the table, we all sat down.

After Richard prayed over our meal, Star asked, "Who wants the first slice of quiche?"

The two boys kept quiet, so I said, "I'll take it."

I saw that both Ned and Roger were watching to see how I would react when I took my first bite.

"Star, this is really tasty. I like it," I said as I went on to take my second bite.

Richard asked for the next slice, and when he tried it, he said, "This is excellent, honey. Come on, boys, try some."

With a big smile on her face, Star dished both boys a slice and when they had taken a bite, they both agreed that it was tasty. They even asked for seconds.

After the tasty breakfast, Richard and the boys went outside to play in the snow. Richard wanted Star to come, but she told him that she had a lot to do to prepare for the Christmas banquet we were going to have.

After Richard and the boys left, I cleared the breakfast dishes, while Star went to prepare the turkey.

As we worked, I said, "I never thanked you for the Bible. I never thought I would even read a Bible, much less own one."

Star came to stand by me and said, "I'm pleased you like it and that you will read it. The Bible is different from any other book. I've been thinking that when I'm here, you and I could have our own Bible study, while Richard spends time with the boys. Would you be willing to do that?"

"Yes, I would. In fact, I was thinking of asking you to do just that. I have a whole lot of questions. It would be a good way to start the new year," I replied.

Star had planned every detail of this banquet; from the traditional turkey and all the trimmings, to stylishly decorating the dining room table in Christmas colors. As I helped put the plates on the table, I realized I had missed a lot growing up. We never had fancy meals at home. Mom was not a cook. She once told me that John was a meat-and-potatoes guy and did not like fancy foods.

If we had something to celebrate, we'd go to a restaurant. When I realized what I was doing, I stopped myself from thinking about the past. I was in a good place now, with a family I loved.

When the guys returned home in the late afternoon, the Christmas banquet was just about ready. Ned was very talkative, telling me about how fast he had gone on his SuperSlider and how he and Roger had raced. He was still telling me about his afternoon when Tex and Dell came in.

Star saw my surprise and said, "Tex and Dell come here every Christmas. It's the only day Dell doesn't have to cook. They've been here for so long, they're like family."

I nodded my head. It felt strange to hear that comment from Star. Then, I remembered that she had known this family a lot longer than I had.

The banquet was a huge success, we all thanked Star for the excellent tasty food she had prepared.

We had finished eating and were having coffee when Tex said, "I got a Christmas card from Neil. He's been gone a long time. He should be finishing his schooling soon."

"Yes, he sent me a card too. He wrote that he'd be back in the spring; he's getting his degree in April," Richard answered.

Ned looked at me and said, "Neil's my uncle. He's going to be a vet. That's an animal doctor." Then, he asked, "Did I ever meet Uncle Neil, Dad?

"No, you were just a baby when he went away," Richard replied. He then went on to ask Tex about the horses.

I was surprised by how little Richard talked about his brother, wondering, *Is there some problem between the two of them?*

After the meal was over and the kitchen cleaned up, we spend a lovely evening playing a game called Sequence. Roger was the best at it. I could see that Ned was tired, and when we found him dozing on the couch, Richard picked him up and carried him to bed. After I tucked Ned into bed, I returned to the living room and said good night to everyone and headed for my apartment.

When I got there, I sat on the edge of my bed, looking at my Bible. I had never opened one before, and when I flipped through it, I found it interesting that it had so many different headings. I laid down and started to read Genesis.

7

When I got to the house the next morning, Richard and Star were having coffee. After we greeted each other, I went to get a coffee, then went to sit by Star.

I saw that she was playing with the ring on her hand, so I asked, "Star, is that a new ring?"

She showed me her hand, and I saw the most beautiful ring.

"Isn't it beautiful?! Richard gave it to me for Christmas. It's my new engagement ring," she answered.

I looked closer and saw the ring had a large diamond surrounded by a cluster of little diamonds. *That is one expensive ring!* I thought.

Before I could say anything, Richard said, "I thought I'd give Star a new ring. We are starting anew in a sense, thanks to you, Trudy."

"You really think I've made that much of a difference?" I asked.

Both Richard and Star nodded their heads.

Richard said, "Ever since you got here, Ned has been a different boy. There is no way Ned would have apologized to Star if he didn't have you in his life."

As he finished speaking, Ned and Roger walked into the dining room. After the boys greeted Richard with a hug, Ned came over to me, gave me a hug and then sat down. He then looked up at me and asked "Mom, would you please make me some pancakes today?"

Dell had been in the kitchen, preparing breakfast for us, but Ned liked it when I made his pancakes.

"Ned, as soon as Dell has put out the food, I'll make you pancakes. Okay?" I said.

Ned nodded his head and sat still waiting patiently for Dell to be done.

Tex joined us at the table as Dell set the food in the warming trays. Once Dell had set out all the food, I went to make Ned his pancakes and when they were done, I brought him his plate.

Once everyone had their plates, Richard said, "I have a big announcement to make."

Everyone at the table looked at him.

He smiled and said, "Star and I have set the date for our wedding. We will get married on Valentine's Day."

He looked at Ned for his reaction, but Ned just continued eating his pancakes, not saying a word.

"Isn't that great, Ned? Your dad and Star are getting married," I said.

He nodded his head and said, "Yeah, it's all right."

I left it at that. At least he was accepting the idea of them getting married.

The holiday week was busy. On New Year's Eve Richard and Star went out with some of their friends. The boys and I stayed home and had a party of our own. We watched *Frozen* and had snacks and sodas.

When we paused the movie for a break, Roger said, "Mom, did you know that it's Ned's birthday tomorrow?"

"Really? Are you going to have a party, Ned?" I asked.

Ned looked at me and said, "Of course. You're making me one."

I gave him a surprised look and said, "Oh, and how would you know that? Why, you little sneak! Were you spying on me?"

He laughed and said, "I know you are because I heard you tell Star. I know about the party, but I don't know what you are planning."

"I wanted it to be a surprise, but the party is tomorrow so I might as well tell you. I rented the pool in town. Liz helped me with the invitations, and all your friends are invited. What do you think of that?" I asked.

He gave a little snicker and said, "Mom, you are the best! Thank you."

After Ned had given me a hug, the three of us returned to watch our movie.

On New Year's Day, Ned's birthday, we left for the pool before Richard and Star had returned home.

Ned was worried that his father was going to miss his party.

After reassuring Ned that Richard would be there, I said, "They are probably waiting for us at the pool. It must have been late when the party ended. They must have stayed at Star's place."

When we got to the pool, sure enough Richard and Star were there. The boys quickly got out of the car, ran to them, and then greeted them with, "Happy New Year!"

As we entered the building, there came a loud cheer, "Surprise! Happy birthday, Ned!"

Ned was so surprised, he just stood still and looked at all the kids there. Then, he looked at me and said, "Oh my! They all came; I think the entire school is here."

Once the kids had changed into their swimsuits, they headed for the pool. I went to changed and joined them while Richard and Star watched from the side lines. We had so much fun playing water games and going down the waterslide. When everyone got tired, we went to change, then we all met in the foyer of the pool to have the birthday cake. When we headed for home, there could not have been a happier kid than Ned. He was grinning from ear to ear. The party had been a huge success.

A few days into the year, on a very cold and snowy day, Richard got a call from Family Services. Jane was calling and asking when the best time would be to meet with all of us. Richard told her that we would all be available the following afternoon. Ned became very quiet; he was a little worried about what the lady would think.

Richard assured him that this lady was on his side and would help him get what he wanted.

The next day we were in a blizzard. Richard tried to call Jane to cancel but was not able to reach her. When we saw Jane's car pull up, we were very surprised.

Richard greeted her at the front door with a warm welcome. After showing her to the living room, where we had a fire going, he introduced her to everyone.

"Would you like something warm to drink? You must be frozen," Star said.

"Oh, that would be wonderful. A coffee would settle my nerves after that drive," Jane answered. She opened her briefcase and took out some papers. "Well, I'm all set, Ned let's start with you. I'm told that you want Trudy to be your real mom. Is that correct?"

Jane had a sweet voice, and Ned liked her instantly. He answered all her questions.

Jane then asked to speak to me. She asked me a series of questions, finally asking why I wanted to become Ned's mother.

I told her that I loved Ned, and I could not see my life without him.

After Jane finished speaking to everyone, she said, "Well, I think I have all the information I need for my report. As soon as I write it up, I'll get it to the judge. The court secretary will call you to set an appointment to see him, but I don't know how long that will take," she said as she replaced all her papers in her briefcase.

When she was ready to go, she said, "I hope the snow drifts have not made the roads impassable."

"You could stay here until the storm passes," Richard said.

"No, I've got an appointment early tomorrow. Goodbye, everyone." Then, she looked at Richard and said, "You have such a loving family. It's nice to see that nowadays."

That night Ned could not settle down. I was sitting on the edge of his bed when he said, "I know that you will be my mom. When I meet the judge, I'll make sure of it. When do you think that sec—you know, the one who Jane said would call us—when do you think she'll call?"

"Oh, you mean the court secretary? Well, I don't know, and worrying about it will not make it happen sooner. Just settle down, Ned. Please get into bed so I can read you a story," I said.

"Trudy, it will be so great, I'll be able to call you Mom all the time and tell everyone that you are my real mom. Won't that be great, Mom? I pray every night that you will be my mom," he said.

I kissed him on the forehead and said, "Yes, Ned, it will be great. Now, do you want me to read to you?"

He nodded.

I hadn't even read a full page when Ned fell fast asleep.

A full month passed before we received the call from the court secretary. It had been a stressful time for all of us. Every day, when I picked up the boys at school, the first thing that Ned asked was if we had received the call.

After supper one night, Ned asked, "Do you think that Jane forgot to give her report to the judge, Dad?"

"Oh, I don't think so. There are a lot of things the judge must deal with. He'll get to our case when it's our turn." Richard assured him.

Ned nodded his head and said, "I hope it will be soon."

Finally, the call came, and an appointment was set for the following Monday. Ned counted off the days on the calendar. The big day finally arrived. Early that morning Ned got up and dressed in the suit his dad had bought him for just this occasion. When I saw him, he looked a miniature of his dad. Ned was so fearful the judge would say no that he could not eat, no matter what I said. He sat at the table and waited for everyone to get ready.

"Is it time to go now? Please, Dad, let's go! We can't be late; the judge would not like that," Ned said.

"Ned, relax. We have plenty of time to get there; the appointment is not till two this afternoon. Let's go have our morning devotions and ask God to be with us today," Richard replied.

We arrived at the courthouse half an hour before the

appointment. We found the judge's office and were directed to a waiting room. A short time later, the judge's assistant came to ask Richard and me to come with her.

Once we were seated in the judge's office, the judge said to Richard, "This is an unusual request, Mr. Lance. Am I to understand that you want your nanny to adopt your son?"

"Yes, sir, that is correct," Richard answered.

The judge looked at him and asked, "How long have you known Miss Rendell?"

Before Richard could answer him, the judge turned to me and said, "Do you know what you are getting into? This is a long-term commitment. Little boys are not puppies."

"Yes, sir, I know," I said. "We've had a lot of discussions about this. Although I've only known Ned a short time, I feel like he *is* my son. I can't explain it, but that is how it feels. The first time he called me Mom, it felt strangely like it was meant to be."

"Do you have more to say, Mr. Lance?" the judge asked.

Richard cleared his throat and said, "Sir, I have been thinking of this since my son asked me if Trudy could adopt him. Ned's mother died when he was born. My mother took care of him till he was three. After that, I hired four nannies, but they all quit because Ned made it impossible for them to care for him. When Trudy applied for the position, it was Ned who said she was hired. From that day on, he has considered her his mother. I know it is unusual, but I think it is the best thing to do for my son. Before Trudy came, I had to break off my engagement to the woman I love because Ned would not have her in the house. Now, with Trudy, we can get married and be a family again."

"What does your fiancée think about this? Do you think it would cause any problem in the future?" the judge asked.

"No, I don't think so. Star is happy to be able to come to the house again, and she is very grateful to Trudy. They get along well," Richard replied.

The judge then turned to me and said, "Miss Rendell, bringing up a child is a lot of work, with many worries. Do you want to take on that kind of responsibility?"

"Yes, sir, I'm aware of that. I already think of Ned as my own," I replied.

"I've read the report from Family Services. I just wanted to hear directly from the two of you," the judge said, then picked up his phone and asked his assistant to have the others come in.

When they were all seated, the judge looked at Ned and said, "You must be Ned."

Ned nodded.

"I hear you want Trudy to be your mother. Is that correct?"

In a soft voice Ned said, "Yes, sir, that is what I want."

After the judge asked Ned a few more questions, he questioned Roger and Star. Once he was satisfied and he had all the information he needed to make his decision, the judge said, "This does not happen often, but I can't find any reasons why I would not grant your petition, young man. Ned, Trudy is now your real mother. I will have the adoption papers drawn up and sent to you in due time."

"Oh, thank you so much, Mr. Judge," Ned said. He then turned to me and gave me the biggest hug ever.

Then, unexpectedly, the judge went to stand by Ned and shook his hand. "Son, you take good care of your mother now. And make sure you listen to her."

Ned was all smiles and promised to do what the judge asked of him.

"That went very well," Richard said as we walked to the restaurant to celebrate.

"I was so scared," Ned said. "That judge was very big, and he was dressed all in black. He was scary."

"You did very well, Ned. It did not show that you were afraid," I said, putting my arm around his shoulder.

We celebrated the adoption at an elegant restaurant. Ned loved sitting in one of those high-back chairs; he said it made him feel like he was a king sitting on a throne.

After the meal, while we were waiting for dessert, Richard raised his water glass and said, "Trudy, as Ned's mother, you are now a big part of this family. We are all happy to have you."

When I went to bed that night, I knew that this day had been very special. I was now the mother of a very lovable little boy, and I thanked God for making it possible. As I closed my eyes, I saw the light again. It was no longer just a glimmer; it was shining brightly.

A few days later, Tex called the house and said Al wanted to talk to me. I had all but forgotten about him. I was a little uneasy about meeting with him. I didn't know what his reaction would be when I told him his bear was in jail. As I opened the door, I greeted him with a smile and asked how he was.

"Oh, I'm good. I'm here for the bear. I'm kind of in a hurry. Would you get it for me quickly?" Al said impatiently.

I smiled and said, "It's not here; we took it to jail. You can get it back when you go pay the bail."

I stepped back when I saw his expression change from impatience to anger.

"You did what? Man!" He yelled as he passed both hands over his hair.

When Richard heard him yell, he came to the door and said, "You heard what Trudy said. The police are having a fund-raiser. All you have to do is pay the bail, then you'll get your bear. Is there a problem with that? The money they raise goes to the children's hospital. You want to help the kids, don't you?"

"Yeah, okay. I'll do that?" Al replied, he turned and went to his car.

As soon as Al left, Richard called the police chief to tell him that Al was back. I wished I could have been there to see what happened to him.

A few mornings later, I saw Al's car in the parking lot in front of the library. I did not give it any thought. When I stopped in front of the school to let the boys out, my driver's door suddenly opened, and Al pushed me to the other side of the car. Roger had gotten out, but Ned was still unbuckling his car seat when Al drove away with me and Ned. I was frightened but could not show Ned that I was.

"What are you doing, Al?" I demanded.

But Al did not reply. He just drove up the road, past the school. Then when he spoke, he said, "I'm holding you and the kid for ransom. I've got to pay this guy for that dope the police have now, thanks to you. If I don't pay him, he's going to kill me. The kid's dad has a lot of dough; he'll pay to get his kid back."

"Al, you can't be serious! This is kidnapping. You could go to jail for the rest of your life for this. Please let us go," I begged.

"I won't hurt the kid; just keep quiet. I need to think," Al replied.

He stopped at a shack a few miles north of the school. Then, he led us inside and told us to sit on the floor.

"Al, it's freezing in here. You can't leave us like this," I protested.

In the middle of the shack there was a small woodstove with a pile of chopped wood beside it.

Al started a fire in it, then said, "There, you have a fire now; you'll be all right till I get back."

He walked out the door and locked us in.

I brought Ned close to me and held him, thankful that Al had not tied us up.

A short time later, the door opened. Much to our surprise, Tex was standing before us. We were so happy to see him; we both ran up to him and hugged him.

"Oh, Tex you came for us, how did you know we were here?" I asked relieved that Tex had come.

"I just came over to see why there was smoke coming out of the chimney. What in the world are you two doing here?" Tex asked in amazement.

"Tex, this bad man kidnapped us and brought us here. Can you call my dad?" Ned asked.

"Where is this guy now?" Tex asked.

"It's Al, you remember him?" I replied. "He said he was going to town to call Richard. He's got my car."

"Come on. We better get you out of here before Al returns. I'll take you home," Tex said as he ushered us out of the shack and helped us get onto the quad.

On our way home Tex radioed Richard to tell him we were safe.

When we got home, Richard was waiting for us. We then learned that Al had already been arrested and a policeman was waiting for us to take our statements.

As the policeman was ready to go, Ned asked, "Will you keep that bad guy in jail?"

"You don't have to worry, young man. This guy will not bother you again. He's going to jail for a long time," the officer said.

That evening we were especially thankful for God's protection. It did not seem to have affected Ned. He had been so brave. Not once had he shown that he was scared, but I was still a little shaken up.

Once Ned was in bed, I went to the living room to watch some TV.

Richard was there, and as I came to sit on one of the La-Z-Boys, he asked, "Are you okay, Trudy?" When I nodded, he continued, "I'm sorry you and Ned had to go through that. When I heard the both of you had been taken, Amanda's accident came to mind. Ned is her little boy, and I don't think I could forgive myself if something bad happened to him. Amanda would have loved him, but she never lived to know him. If she had lived, things would be so different for us."

Yes, that's for sure. I would not be here, I thought.

"Things have changed so much. Now I love Star. I never thought I'd ever love anyone but Amanda. She was my first love. It's so strange," Richard said, more to himself than to me. He was in an odd mood. He looked at me and then continued, "The pain of losing her never goes away. It will be with me for the rest of my life, I suppose. But, you know, it's a little different now. I can speak of her without crying."

I looked at him and wondered why he was telling me these things.

"Yes, I know how that feels. It's so painful losing someone you love," I replied.

I don't think he even heard what I said, for he then said, "I wonder what Amanda thinks about me marrying Star. But I have to go on with my life; I can't dwell on the past. Amanda is my past, and Star is my future."

He got up and said, "Good night, Trudy. Sleep well. God bless."

After he left, I sat for a while, thinking of what he had said. I wondered if my mother had those kinds of feelings when she married John. She used to tell me that she had loved my father very much, but I couldn't remember her telling me that she loved John. I had never thought of that before. As Richard had said, "It's so strange."

With a week left until Valentine's Day, Star and I finished with the last touches of the renovations Star had done in the master bedroom. After Richard and Tex had moved all the furniture out of the room, Star had hired painters to repaint the entire room. The rug had been steam-cleaned; now all we needed was the new furniture. The first time I set foot in the room, I was surprised by how spacious it was. The room was a suite, consisting of a large bedroom, a smaller sitting room with patio doors leading to a patio, and a humongous bathroom. The master bath had a large jetted tub set into one corner. There was a walk-in shower, with dual shower heads, in the opposite corner. The sides of the shower were covered with tiny blue glass tiles that sparkled when the light was turned on. The bathroom vanity had two sinks and ran along the wall on the same side of the room as the shower.

We were hanging the new curtains to cover the patio windows when Star said, "Well, I'm glad to be finishing up the remodeling. Once the furniture gets here, Richard can have his bedroom back. I hope he likes what I've done."

"This is a very lovely room. You did a wonderful job matching the color in the curtains with the color of the walls. I like it," I said.

"Yes, I agree. For a while I was a little concerned that the curtains would be all wrong, but it all turned out just perfect. Richard has been so good to me, letting me change the room like I wished. I do hope he likes it," Star replied.

"What are you going to use the little room for? I guess it would be nice as a reading room," I said.

"I'm going to make a nursery out of it when we have a baby. Richard said that Amanda used it as a dressing room," Star replied.

"Has Richard ever said anything to you about Amanda?" I asked, then, thinking this might not be the right thing to ask Star, I said, "I'm sorry. It's not really my concern, I'm just asking for Ned's sake."

"Has Richard told you about Amanda?" Star asked in return.

"He told me about the way she died and Ned's birth. That's about all," I replied, then added, "I suppose that's all he wants me to know."

"Well, Trudy, you are Ned's mother now, and it's only natural you would want to know about your son's mother. I'll sit Richard down tonight, and we'll ask him," Star said.

"Oh, I don't know about that. He might think I'm a little to nosy," I said.

"I don't think it's nosy. Besides, I'd like to know more about Richard's life with Amanda," Star replied.

After the boys were in bed, we were all in the living room, talking about how our day had gone when Star asked, "Richard, would you tell us about Amanda?"

Richard looked surprised by the question and said, "You want to know about Amanda? Why?"

"Richard, I just want to know about your life before I met you and how this Lance family got started. Is that okay? I think Trudy would also love to hear about Ned's mother," Star replied.

Richard laughed and said, "Okay, what would you like to know?"

Star turned to me and said, "Go ahead, Trudy, ask the first question."

I hesitated a second, surprised by what Star had just done.

"Would you tell us how the two of you met?" I said, a little nervous asking Richard such a question.

He looked at both of us and said, "Amanda worked in the store where I bought my clothes. It was the only store that sold the cowboy shirts I liked. Every time I went into her store, she would come to help me. She was a little flirty, with her smile and the little laugh she had. I guess it was her way of telling me that she liked me, but I was clueless. One day we met at the food court in the mall, and she asked me if I would join her for lunch. I was still clueless. The next time I saw her, she bumped into me. After she said she was sorry, she asked me if I had seen the new *Superman* movie. I said no, so she asked me if I would like to go see it with her. I said I'd love to. After the movie, we went for coffee at Tim's. That's when I clued in. I told her to let me ask her for the next date."

"Ah, were you the shy type, huh, Richard?" Star teased.

"Yeah, I suppose. I'm a cowboy and never had much contact with the lady folks," Richard said in a joking way. Then, he got serious again and continued, "I never thought a lady like Amanda would ever look at me, let alone want to marry me. I was twenty-five years old and still lived in the same house I grew up in. Amanda showed me that I needed to make a change."

"Were you happy with Amanda?" Star asked.

Richard smiled and said, "Yes, Star, I was. We had a good life together. But that was then. Now it's you and me, my love. Let's talk about something else. How are the wedding plans coming along?"

8

Star wanted a simple wedding, just close friends and family. Dell volunteered to cater the supper. Arrangements were made to have the preacher from the church come to the house to perform the ceremony. Star's dress, which she had specially ordered more than two years before, was secretly stored in my apartment. She told me that when they put off the wedding, she did not think that she would ever wear the dress.

The day before the wedding I was alone with the boys. We had planned to surprise Richard and Star by decorating the living room for their wedding. So, in the afternoon the boys and I made heart-shaped streamers and hung them over the archway that led into the living room. We made large hearts in red cardboard paper and hung them all around the room. The boys made a large heart with Richard's name on it and interlocked it with a heart the same size with Star's name on it. These were placed over two chairs that had been decorated as thrones. It took us all afternoon and into the evening before we had finished.

As we stepped back to admire our creation, Ned said, "What do you think Dad will say? He doesn't like mushy stuff much, you know."

Roger looked at what we had done and said, "Oh, I think he'll like this. He's very happy to be marrying Star. Have you noticed that he is always smiling these days?"

"Yeah, I noticed. I guess Star makes him happy. Do you think when she moves here and lives here all the time things will be different?" Ned asked.

"We'll have to give her a chance. Things might be a little different, but I know one thing. Dad will be a lot happier, and if he's happy, he'll be nicer to us," Roger replied.

"I'll be nice to Star. What do you think I should call her? Will 'Miss Star' be okay, Mom?" Ned asked.

I was cleaning up some cardboard and not expecting that question, but I replied, "I think that would be all right. Just be nice."

I had listened to what the boys were saying and was relieved to hear that Ned would be all right with Star moving here.

It was getting late and tomorrow was going to be a big day, so I said, "I think we are all finished here. The decorations look lovely. I think your dad and Star are going to be very surprised. Ned, it's time for you to go brush your teeth. Roger, will you help me with this ladder?"

After Roger and I had put the ladder away, I went to Ned's room. He was already in bed, waiting for me to read him a story.

When I finished reading, Ned asked, "Mom, what do you think it will be like when Star comes to live with us?"

"Oh, I think it will be good," I said. "Star is very nice, and she loves your father very much. And you know what else?"

Ned looked at me and said, "What?"

I sensed he was expecting me to tell him a big secret, but all I said was "She loves you too. You should try to love her back."

"Oh yes. I'll try," Ned replied. Then, he reached up to give me a huge hug and said, "Mom, I love you. You are the best!"

I kissed his forehead and replied, "Love you too, my boy. You have a good sleep."

On Valentine's Day, when Ned came in the kitchen, he was surprised to see a big chocolate heart in place of his cereal bowl. When he saw it, I was surprised to see that he was very quiet. I thought that he'd be excited about the valentine that I had given him, but he had the saddest face.

"Ned, what's wrong?" I asked.

"I forgot to make you a valentine, Mom. All the hearts we made, and I did not even make one for you. It's the first Valentine's Day that I have a mom, and I forget to give you a valentine. I'm sorry," he said.

"It's okay, Ned," I replied.

But he looked at me with those green eyes and said, "No, it's not."

"Well, Ned, it's going to be Valentine's Day all day. If you think you must give me one, why don't you make one?" I said.

With that, he jumped up and said, "I'll be right back, Mom."

He ran in the direction of his room and was gone for a time. When he returned to the kitchen, he was carrying a large card. On it was a heart with an arrow through it. The words below read, "Be My Valentine."

Roger was standing behind Ned and together they said, "It's from both of us."

"What is all this? Doesn't anybody know that I'm getting married today? Where's my breakfast? What's all this mushy stuff?" Richard said as he came into the kitchen behind the boys.

Richard had the biggest smile on his face. Both boys turned to hug their father.

"We would have made you a valentine too, Dad, but we know you don't like this mushy stuff," Ned said.

With that, Richard picked Ned up, gave him a big bear hug, and kissed the top of his head.

"I'll show you mushy stuff, boy! How do you like that?" Richard said as he gave him another huge hug.

Ned was not able to breathe for a second.

"Dad, Dad, you're choking me. Okay, it's mushy enough," Ned said between gasps.

As they played, I went to get their breakfast. Dell was busy making food for the wedding, so I oversaw breakfast.

As we ate breakfast, Ned asked, "Where is Star?"

"I don't know. I'm surprised she's not here by now, but I'm not supposed to see her till the wedding. Trudy, would you know when she's supposed to arrive?" Richard said.

"She should be here any minute now; she said she would be here by nine." I looked at the time and continued, "And it's a quarter after. I'll go see if she's in the apartment. That's where she will be getting ready."

When I got to the apartment, there was no sign of Star. I returned to the house and told Richard that she wasn't there.

Richard's smile was quickly replaced by a big frown. He tried her cell, and when he got no answer, he said, "What could have happened to her? I'll send Tex to drive down the road. Maybe she had car trouble."

A short time later, we saw Tex drive up, with Star in the passenger seat.

Richard was so relieved to see her that he ran out to meet them, with all of us right behind him.

When Star saw Richard, she said, "You're not supposed to see me till the wedding."

"Oh, never mind about that, Star! Are you all right?" Richard asked as he held her in his arms.

"Yes, I'm all right. I hit this big pothole and wrecked the tire. I just did not see it. I was in the middle of changing the tire when Tex drove up. I was so glad to see him. I tried to call, but there's no cell coverage in that area," Star said as we all went into the house.

When we were all inside, Star turned to Richard and said, "Now, let's get this wedding going. I should be ready in an hour. The pastor and our guests will be here soon. Trudy, come. I'll need your help."

As she sat down on the couch in my apartment, Star said, "I'm so nervous, and hitting that pothole sure did not help. I should have paid more attention. See? I'm still shaking."

"I'll go get you a nice cup of my herbal tea, the one you like," I said. "Do you want anything to eat?"

"Just some dry toast," Star replied, "And, yes, that tea would be perfect."

When I returned with the tea and toast, Star was just getting out of the shower. It was then I saw that she had draped her dress over the couch. With her hair in a towel, she came to sit at the table and ate the toast and sipped the tea. Once she had finished, she went to dry her hair, then returned to sit at the table and said, "Trudy would you be able to curl my hair in the back. I've done the front, but I can never manage the back."

As I curled her hair, I asked, "How did you and Richard meet?"

"Richard and I met at a support group I was volunteering with. I was in charge of making coffee and tea. I had seen Richard there, but we had not spoken. Then, one night, I saw him sitting all alone, so I went to sit by him and introduced myself. Initially, we just talked about the weather or things we had heard on the news. It's a long story, but the short version is that we fell in love, and here we are today. It seems I've been waiting for this day for a long time. I was starting to lose hope we'd ever get married, but you made it possible. Thanks, Trudy," Star said.

"You're welcome. I think there was someone watching over all of us," I replied.

"Yes, you are right about that. God has been so good to us," she said.

After I finished with her hair, Star put on her makeup. Then with my help she put on her wonderful wedding dress. As she looked in the full-length mirror, she asked, "How do I look? Do you think Richard will like the dress?"

"You look marvelous, Star. Richard will love it," I replied.

The dress Star wore was a white satin dress, with the bodice and long sleeves covered with fine lace. It had a straight skirt with a short train in the back. Star looked very elegant in it, and it complimented her tall, slim figure very well. Because it was a house wedding, she had decided not to wear a veil. As we walked out of the apartment, she carried a single red rose.

When we stepped into the house, everyone turned to look at us.

Richard came to her, kissed her, and said, "Oh my! You do look wonderful. Will you marry me?"

Star smiled and said, "Of course, Mr. Lance, that's why we're here. No more delays. Let's get married."

"All right. This lady wants to marry me. Pastor, please marry us before she changes her mind," Richard said.

Everyone followed them to the living room, and when we got there, Richard and Star went to stand before the chairs the boys had decorated as thrones. There, they said the vows they had written to each other and exchanged rings.

After the pastor pronounced them husband and wife, he said, "Please welcome Mr. and Mrs. Richard Lance. Richard, you may kiss your bride."

They kissed, and when they broke off the kiss, I saw Richard's face change. I looked in the direction he was looking and saw what looked like a younger version of Richard.

Star also saw the change of expression on his face and asked, "Richard, what's the matter?"

"Neil is here! My brother!" he said.

He took Star's hand, and they went to greet Neil.

"You came! It's so great to see you here," Richard said, giving Neil a hug.

"You think I would miss your wedding, Richard? Are you going to introduce me to your lovely new bride?" Neil asked.

After Richard had introduced them, Star said, "Hello, Neil, what a wonderful surprise. Richard has told me about you, but I was starting to wonder if he had made you up. I'm very pleased to finally meet you."

When she extended her hand to shake Neil's, he took her hand and gently pulled her into a hug.

I saw Ned and Roger go to stand beside their father, so I went to stand behind Ned.

After hugging Star, Neil turned to the boys. He put his hands on Rogers shoulders and said, "Roger, my goodness, how have you grown!" Then, he turned to Ned and as he gave him a hug, said, "And you must be Ned. You're not a baby anymore."

"Yes, Uncle Neil, I'm Ned, and this is my mom."

Never had I seen anyone look so surprised. I knew Neil was trying to make sense of what Ned had just told him, so I said, "Hello, Neil. I'm Trudy."

"Trudy? How can you be Ned's mother?" he asked.

Before I could answer, Ned replied, "Trudy adopted me. The judge said she's my real mom now."

Neil looked at Richard, then asked, "Richard, why would you let this happen?"

"Neil, I'll fill you in on what has happened later. Come. Let's celebrate my marriage to Star," Richard said.

Champagne was served, and when everyone had a glass, Tex came to stand beside the newlyweds. He raised his glass and said, "To Richard and Star; to new beginnings."

Everyone echoed, "To new beginnings."

Neil was standing at Richard's side and said, "Yes, to Richard and Star. Welcome to the Lance family, Star. May you be very happy together."

I noticed that Neil had his eye on me as he toasted the newlyweds.

"Thank you, Neil. I'm very happy that you are here; it makes this day so much more special," Richard replied.

Once the toasts were over, the guests came to congratulate Richard and Star and offered them their good wishes.

Dell was the last to offer her wishes, and right after that, Richard said, "Dell has informed me that the banquet is ready. Let's all go to the dining room."

Richard and Star led the way to the dining room, and when we got there, Richard helped Star with her chair. He went to sit at the head of the table, while Neil went to sit at the opposite end. Roger, Ned, and I sat to Richard's left. After all the guests were seated, Dell and her helper brought in the food. First, we were served a green salad with a delicious dressing. The salad was followed by beef Wellington, with Yorkshire pudding, small potatoes, gravy, and baby peas. I'd never had a tastier meal. Everyone complimented Dell on the delicious food.

After we finished eating the main course, Dell brought in a heart-shaped wedding cake with bright-red icing. The newlyweds' names were written on the top in white icing. After Richard and Star made the first cut and a piece was removed, I saw that it was a red velvet cake. I'd never had that kind of cake before, but when I tasted it, I found it to be delicious.

During the meal I felt like I was being watched; whenever I looked in Neil's direction, he would look away.

By late afternoon, the only guests remaining were Liz and her family.

I was talking to Liz and Star when Neil came by and said, "Star, how does it make you feel when Ned calls the nanny Mom?"

Richard was at Star's side in a flash. He looked at his brother and said, "Neil, I told you that I would tell you later. Why would you ask Star that? Are you here to cause trouble?"

"Richard, I'm sorry. I should not have asked that. I'm sorry, Star," Neil replied, slurring his words.

"Neil, have you been drinking? You'd best go sober up, brother. When you're sober, we'll tell you what happened while you were gone," Richard said firmly.

With his head down, Neil turned and left the room.

I was thankful that Ned and Roger had not witnessed that encounter.

Later in the evening, while Ned and I were sitting on the couch in the living room, Neil walked in and asked, "May I join you?"

He sat next to Ned before I could answer. *Oh, I hope you have sobered up.* I thought. *I don't want you to destroy Ned's idea of you.*

Neil got closer to Ned and said, "Ned, you have grown since I last saw you. You were just a baby then, no longer than my arm. How old are you now?"

"I'm six. I don't remember you, Uncle Neil, but Dad told me about you. I'm glad you came to Dad's wedding," Ned replied.

Neil turned to look at me and asked, "Tell me, Trudy, what brought you here?"

But before I could answer, Ned replied, "Jesus brought Trudy here to be my mother."

"Oh, He did, did He?" Neil replied.

I could see he was a little taken aback. He looked at me, and I saw that he wanted to ask something else but stopped himself. I smiled but did not say anything. He made me a little uncomfortable with those green eyes of his.

I turned to Ned and said, "I think it's time for bed. It's getting late, and you've had a long day."

"Uncle Neil, we can talk tomorrow right? How long will you be here?" Ned asked.

"Yes, Ned, we can talk tomorrow. Now have a good night," Neil replied as he reached over and tousled Ned's hair.

We went to find Richard and Star to say good night. They were in the kitchen, talking to Dell and Tex. When Ned saw his dad, he ran to him.

Richard pulled Ned into his arms and said, "Good night, son. You were very grown up today. I love you." He gave Ned a kiss, then set him down.

Ned turned to Star and said, "Good night, Miss Star. I'm happy you married my dad. You make him very happy."

Star bent down, kissed Ned on the forehead, and said, "Thank you for saying that, Ned. I love your dad very much, and I also love you."

"Ned, remember what we told you. Star and I are leaving tonight. We'll be gone for a week," Richard reminded Ned.

"Yes, Dad, I remember. Mom said you're going on your honeymoon," Ned replied.

After I tucked Ned into bed, I went downstairs. As I walked

by the living room archway, Richard saw me and asked me to join them.

When I walked into the living room, I saw Star sitting on the couch and Neil sitting on one of the La-Z-Boys. I went to sit on the other La-Z-Boy, and Richard went to join Star.

"I've asked Trudy to join us. I think she should know what happened to this family too," Richard said. Then, he turned to Neil and said, "Neil, it's really good to have you home. How have you been? I haven't heard from you in five years. Why did you stay away for so long? Why didn't you return my calls? Who told you I was getting married?"

"Whoa, Richard, one question at a time." Neil paused for a second, then said, "Richard, I just wanted to forget what happened. Every time you called, it brought back all the bad memories of Amanda and Jill and how our lives got all botched up. I didn't know how to deal with that, so I ignored your calls. I'm sorry I did that. I kept in touch with Tex, though. He's the one who told me you were getting married."

Richard looked at Neil with compassion and said, "I'm sorry too, brother."

There was an odd pause as both brothers looked at each other.

Then, in a soft voice Neil asked, "How did you and Star meet?"

"That, my brother, is a long story. Star saved me from who knows what. You know I was a nut job after Amanda died. It got worse after you left. Mom was caring for the boys and wanted me to be more involved with them, but I was so lost in my bottle I didn't bother. But Mom would not let me be. She hounded me day after day for months. She'd take as many of my bottles as she could find and poured the contents down the drain, and then she kept asking me to go to AA meetings. After a while, I got tired of her nagging, so I gave in. I remember the first time I attended a meeting. I was like a little boy. She took my hand and led me up the stairs, then, once at the door, she pushed me into the hall and told me to sit down. At first, I would just sit there and try not to listen to the drunks. I heard how they had lost their families and their jobs. All I could think was, *Why don't you stop drinking, you loser?* After a while, it dawned on me: I was one of those losers. That night when I got home, I took a drink. It tasted so bad, it made me want to puke. I took all the bottles and poured the contents down the drain. I haven't had a single drink since," Richard said.

He looked at Star, smiled at her, then continued. "But I kept going to the AA meetings. After one of those meetings, I was sitting at a table in the cafeteria when this lady, Star, walked in and came to sit at the table where I was sitting. She asked why I came to the meetings. I told her I came because my mother made me come."

He looked at Star again and started to laugh. "Star looked at me and said, 'Really? You're a grown man. I don't think anyone can make you do anything. I think you come because you know that you need help.' That made me realize that I did need help, so that's when I started to see a psychiatrist."

Richard looked at Neil and continued, "Once I was in therapy, I stopped going to the meetings and did not see Star again until we met at a school meeting. There was talk of closing the school. Star was there to represent the school in town. After the meeting, I asked her if we could go for coffee. She told me that she hadn't eaten all day and asked me if I would come have dinner with her instead. As we ate, I told her how I was doing, then asked her if I could take her to a movie that weekend. When we got to the movie, I could see that the movie made her very uncomfortable, so we walked out. As I drove her home, she told me that she was a Christian and asked me what I believed. When I told her that I had never thought about it much, I thought that Star would not be for me. I took her home and told her I'd call her."

Richard stopped talking and again looked at Star. He brought her close and kissed her.

"But, you know, Neil, I could not get her out of my mind. I would think of her all the time, so I called her one night and told her that. To my surprise, Star told me that she could not stop thinking of me either. We started seeing each other. Over time and after many questions about her faith, I became a Christian," Richard said with gladness in his face.

"You're a Christian? I can't believe that. You were always your own man; you never needed anyone or anything. Star sure did a number on you," Neil said.

Richard gave a small laugh and said, "Star told me about her faith and what she believed. Oh no, Neil, it wasn't Star's doing. It was the Holy Spirit who drew me to Jesus, and I willingly accepted His gift of salvation. I have peace now instead of anger. I can love again. Star was a gift from God."

I saw that Neil was having trouble believing what Richard had just told him. He shook his head and said, "Well, dear brother, that is quite the story. I'll have to digest what you said. And what about Ned's mother?"

Neil looked at me, then turned to Richard and asked, "How could you let the nanny adopt your son?"

Richard took a breath and said, "Trudy became Ned's mother for the sake of Ned's well-being."

Richard then recounted what Ned had been like before I arrived.

When Richard finished, Neil said, "Well, I certainly can't imagine Ned behaving that way. He seems like a nice little boy." He paused, then said, "Don't you and Star have to go catch a plane and start your honeymoon?"

"Yes, we'll have to go soon. I'm glad we had this talk," Richard replied.

"Yes, thank you for telling me. I'll be gone when you come back, but I'll be returning home for good in April, after I finish my studies. I'll have a big surprise for you then," Neil said with a big smile on his face.

"What kind of surprise?" Richard asked in a concerned voice.

"Oh, don't worry, big brother, you'll like it. I think," Neil replied.

After we wished Richard and Star a good journey, they left on their honeymoon, leaving me with Neil and the boys.

"Well, Trudy, what do we do now? What does a nanny do when the kids are asleep?" Neil asked.

I looked at him, trying to figure out if he was being serious. When I did not answer right away, he turned and left the living room.

I was watching the news when he returned with a beer in his hand. He sat in the chair next to me and said, "Oh, I should have asked you if you'd like a beer."

"No thank you, Neil. I'm going to bed. Good night," I said.

I was just about out of the room when he asked, "Trudy, where will you be sleeping?"

I gave him a questioning look.

When he saw the look, he laughed and said, "Trudy, I just want to know so that I don't go to the same room."

"Oh. I'll be in the guest room next to Ned's room. I usually stay in the apartment, but since Richard will not be here, we thought it would be better for me to be closer to the boys," I replied.

"Trudy, you don't have to worry. I wouldn't disturb you. I'll find a place to lay my head. Good night," he replied.

"Good night, Neil. Will you lock up?" I asked.

Neil nodded.

I nodded back and left the room. I was so relieved to be away from him. All that had been a little too awkward.

As I laid in bed I thought, *They might look alike, but Neil sure isn't the gentleman his brother is.*

9

The boys and I were having breakfast, when Neil walked into the kitchen. He greeted us and went to get a cup of coffee.

"Uncle Neil, do you want to have some pancakes. Mom made them. She makes the best pancakes. Right, Roger?" Ned asked.

"Yes, Ned, she does," Roger replied and continued to eat.

Neil went to get a plate from the sideboard then came to sit beside Ned, and asked, "How many have you had?"

Ned gave him a big smile and said, "I had four. Roger had five. How many are you going to have, Uncle Neil?"

Neil looked at me and said, "Well, if they're as tasty as you say, I'll have four too."

I passed Neil the plate of pancakes, and he helped himself to four of them. As he ate, he asked, "So, boys, do you have big plans for today?"

"No, Uncle Neil, not really," Ned replied, then asked me, "Mom, do we have plans?"

"We have to put all the decorations from the wedding away. After that, we have no plans," I answered.

"Would you help us, Uncle Neil?" Ned asked.

"Sure, Ned, I can. Besides, it's awful outside. I was hoping to go cross-country skiing, but with this rain, the snow would not be very good. Maybe once the rain let's up, we could go see the old house."

"Really, Uncle Neil? I've only been in it once. Dad never lets us play in there. He said that it was your house," Ned informed his uncle.

After lunch, the rain stopped, so we joined Neil on a hike to the old house, following a path through the pine trees. I was surprised by how close the old house was to the main house when taking this path. When we got there, Neil unlocked the door and pushed it open. I could tell no one had been in the house for a long time when a musty smell assailed us as we entered. The house had been built in the sixties and needed a great deal of updates, but it had character, with its big stone fireplace and hardwood floors in the living room and dining room.

The minute I stepped into the kitchen, I was brought back to my childhood. My mother had the similar green fridge, green stove, and white-and-green tile floor. As I looked around, I said, "This kitchen sure needs a good remodeling."

"Oh, what's wrong with it? Don't you like the green? It was *the* thing in the seventies," Neil replied in a serious tone. Then, he laughed and asked the boys if they liked green appliances.

Both Ned and Roger thought that green appliances were better than plain white ones.

After touring most of the house, we ended up in Neil's study. As we entered the room, we found an entire wall covered with ribbons and trophies.

"Oh my! Uncle Neil, are these all yours?" Ned asked as he went closer to look at them.

"They sure are. I joined 4-H Canada when I was ten. Dad would give me a calf in the spring, and over the summer, I would spend all my time taking care of it. In the fall my dad and I would go to fairs, and I'd show my calf." He walked over to the ribbons, picked up a golden one, and said, "This is the first ribbon I won. I was happy to win the other ribbons, but this one is the one I value the most."

I could see that Ned was impressed.

As the boys continued admiring the trophies, Neil's phone rang. When he ended his call, he looked at the boys and said, "Well, my flight has been canceled. There's a big storm at the airport, and everything is shut down. You guys are stuck with me for another day."

Both boys were delighted with the news.

As we were returning to the main house, Neil asked, "Ned, what do you think of my house?"

Ned looked him in the eye and replied, "It's okay, Uncle Neil, but I don't like the way it smells."

Neil had a good laugh, then said, "Yeah, I agree. How about we go see the horses? Tex told me your dad bought a new mare. I'd like to take a look at it."

The boys spent the rest of the afternoon with their uncle and returned to the house just as I was getting supper out of the oven.

As we ate, I noticed that Ned was unusually quiet, so when we were finished eating, I asked, "Ned, did you have a good time with your uncle? I think it has tired you out."

"Yeah, Mom, I did. It was fun to be with Uncle Neil. Can we have ice cream for dessert?" he replied.

After dessert, Ned asked Neil to come see the Legos he had built.

I cleaned up the supper dishes then went to see how they were doing. When I got to Ned's room, I found him in bed, fast asleep. There was no sign of Neil.

With Ned and Roger in bed and the kitchen tidied up, I went to the living room to watch TV. I was curled up on one of the La-Z-Boys when Neil walked into the room.

"Oh, there you are. What are you watching?" he asked as he sat in the other chair.

"Just some love story, a chick flick. You wouldn't like it," I replied.

He frowned and said, "Oh, you know what I like to watch now, do you?"

"No, but in general, guys don't like this type of movie. That's all I meant. I can change the channel," I said.

"No, no. I happen to be an old romantic. I like love stories, like Richard and Star's story," he replied.

We sat watching the movie, not saying a word until the commercial break, and then he said, "Trudy, I know how Ned behaved before you came and how he has changed since you came, but why would you agree to be Ned's mother?"

I was surprised that he would still have concerns about me adopting Ned. After thinking a while about how I was going to answer, I said, "Neil, I had to think long and hard before making that decision. Over time it became clear to me that being Ned's mother was the reason why I came here. The first time I saw Ned, I told him he was the most wonderful little boy I had ever seen. When he asked me to be his mother, it felt a little strange, but I somehow knew it was what I was meant to do. He loves me, and I love him." I hoped that it did not seem too weird to him.

He nodded his head and then asked, "Are you a Christian too?"

"No, I'm not," I replied, but I realized in that moment that I did want to be one.

We continued to watch the movie in silence.

When the movie ended, I asked, "Neil, can I ask you a question?"

"Well, I guess it's only fair, since I questioned you. Go ahead and ask," Neil replied.

"Who is Jill?" I asked.

When he heard the question, he seemed to recoil. I thought that he was not going to answer, but he said, "Jill? Jill is Amanda's sister."

"Oh, was she at the accident? Were you there? Richard told me about the accident but never told me any details," I replied and then added, "Neil, if you don't want to tell me, you don't have to. I shouldn't have asked. I'm sorry."

"Trudy, that night changed everyone in this family. I've never spoken about it to anyone. It's like a bad secret I can't tell anyone. But I see that's not what I should be doing. Richard has gone on with his life, he dealt with what happened, but I don't think I have. I just buried myself in my studies and never allowed myself to think about it," he replied.

He looked so sad. I was about to say good night and leave the room, but he continued, "Yes, I was there. Jill was there too. Maybe I'll start with when I first met her. We met at Richard and Amanda's wedding. Jill was my age, so pretty—gorgeous, in fact—and she knew that she was. She was the biggest flirt. The first time I saw her, I fell in love. We met again when Jill came to spend the summer with Amanda here on the ranch. Jill and I became lovers the summer we finished high school. At the end of the summer, I headed to university, and we said goodbye. When I asked Jill to keep in touch, she told me that it had only been a summer fling and wouldn't return my calls. I was crushed. I had really fallen for her, but she acted like nothing had happened between us. We got together again the next summer. At the end of the summer, she told me that she was pregnant, and we'd have to get married. I loved her, but I had five more years of school. I knew it was going to be hard, but I agreed, so we got married. We had never talked about a future together. By summer's end I was set to go back to school, telling her I had rented an apartment for us. It was then she told me she did not want me to go back to school but to stay with her here at the ranch. We had the biggest fight. She also informed me that she was not pregnant and would never want to have any babies with me. After the fight, she treated me as if I did not exist. I went back to school and never returned to the ranch until the summer holidays."

Neil paused and then resumed the story. "When I returned, Jill treated me a little better. But I saw her in a different light. Jill wanted everything her sister had. Amanda had this new house, so Jill wanted me to build her a new house. Amanda got a new car, so Jill had to have one too. When Amanda got pregnant with Ned, I found that Jill became very friendly toward me again. When I told her I would not get her pregnant, she got very upset with me, so I left for school three weeks early. Over the months that followed we reconciled, so I returned home for the holidays. We were at a New Year's Eve party with Richard and Amanda when Amanda said she was tired and wanted to go home. She was only days away from her due date. Richard and I were in the middle of a big poker game, so when Jill volunteered to drive her sister home, we agreed. After the game ended, we headed for home. We were just about home when we saw flashing red lights. We rounded the curve and came upon the accident. When we saw the car, Richard got out before I could come to a stop. He ran toward the car, yelling Amanda's name. The police tried to stop him, but he just pushed them aside, still yelling her name. When I got to the car, I saw Amanda on a stretcher, with an EMT working to revive her. The EMT informed Richard that his wife had passed but that he could save the baby. So they performed a caesarean and took Ned out of her. I will always remember his cry: so loud, like he was angry. When the ambulance left, we both looked at Jill. She must have seen that we were blaming her for the accident because she said, 'This was an accident. Amanda is my sister; I would never hurt her. It was an accident.' She turned and ran toward home. Richard wanted to go to the hospital to be with the baby and say a proper goodbye to Amanda, so I drove him to town. We never returned home until the next morning. I searched for Jill, but she was nowhere to be found. After the police investigated the accident, they told us that there had been black ice on the road, and because of it, the car had no traction to make the curve. The car hit a big tree, totaling the passenger side."

Neil stopped and just looked at me, shaking his head.

"That is so awful, Neil. I'm so sorry your family had to go through all of that. I wonder if it has affected Ned—I mean, the way he was born. I wonder if that was why he felt he needed to have a mom," I said.

"You are very dedicated to that little boy, aren't you?" Neil asked.

"Yes, I am. He is my son now. I'm his mother. I love him very much. Can I ask you one more question?" I asked.

Neil nodded his head, so I asked, "Are you still married?"

"Yes, I am. I thought of getting a divorce many times, but I don't even know where Jill went. She could be dead, for all I know. All she ever did was give me grief. I put all my effort and energy into my studies and tried not to think of her," he replied in the saddest voice.

"Thank you for telling me, Neil," I said.

"Well, it is what it is. I think it's time to hit the sack; I have a long day tomorrow. Good night, Trudy," Neil said as he got up and walked out of the room.

Now that I knew what he had gone through, I saw Neil in a different light. I sat for a while, thinking about all that he had told me. The things that had happened to this family were terrible. I noticed how differently the two brothers had dealt with their loss. Richard had drowned his sorrow by drinking, while Neil had buried himself in his studies.

I then thought, *And how did I deal with my loss? I went into a deep, dark depression.*

When I got to bed and opened my Bible, I remembered the question Neil had asked me: "Are you a Christian?" After attending church at Christmas, I had started going to church with the family. Many times, the pastor had asked if anyone wanted to accept Jesus, but I had never responded. I always thought I needed to know more before I decided; however, tonight, I knew I had to make the decision I had put off. I realized that I believed in Jesus and that I had faith in Him and trusted Him.

I knelt beside my bed and said, "Jesus, please come into my life and be my Lord. I turn from my sins, and I ask for Your forgiveness. From now on, I want to be a child of Yours. Thank you, Jesus, for making me Yours."

There, Lord. I have committed my life to You, now what do I do? I thought, realizing how little I knew about God. Then, I thought, *I have my Bible, my studies with Star, and Star and Richard to teach me.*

A hunger stirred up inside me; I just had to get to know Him. Before I got off my knees, I remembered the way Ned prayed every night, so I thanked God for bringing me here and asked Him to help Neil to find His peace. And then, just as I had every night since becoming Ned's mother, I prayed that God would keep my son safe, and I thanked God for him.

As I laid in bed, I remembered the light I had seen when I first came here. It had grown, now it burned brightly.

We were all very happy when Star and Richard returned from their honeymoon. After we greeted them, we went to sit at the dining room table to catch up on the week's activities.

Ned did the most talking; he told Richard all about what they had done with Neil and how much they had missed him after he left.

After Ned finished recounting all his news, Richard asked me how my week had gone.

"It went very well. We had no problems," I replied.

Ned then very unexpectedly said, "Mom has accepted Jesus."

I smiled at Ned and said, "Yes, that's right. I finally surrendered to the Lord."

"What great news! Trudy, I'm so happy for you," Richard said.

As Star came to give me a hug, I said, "But I still have a lot of questions. You'll get tired of me asking you."

"I'll be only too pleased to answer them. You are now my sister in the Lord," Star said.

It felt so good to hear her say that. I always wanted a sister.

Star took her place in the family as the mistress of the household. At first, things stayed the same, except for the music. Star always had music playing in whatever room she was in. I liked listening to it. Star said it was praise-and-worship music. It sure wasn't like the country music John had played while I was growing up.

Star had kept her apartment in town and had moved only her personal things to the ranch. Over time I noticed little changes: a tablecloth on the dining room table, pictures on the mantel, and houseplants. I loved the Norfolk pine she placed in the corner of the living room where the Christmas tree had been. For some reason, Richard never had plants in the house. My guess was that he did not want the hassle of watering them.

The biggest change Star made was the food. Every week, we had a new dish we had not tried before. Dell still cooked, but the menu ideas were Star's. Star would help Dell do the cooking, but she never took credit, always praising Dell for the excellent meal.

For me, the best thing about having Star at the ranch was the changes she brought to my life. She became my close friend and mentor. I loved the time we shared, whether just talking or studying the Bible.

One evening as I was tucking Ned into bed, he asked, "Did you like supper tonight? I ate so much I thought I was going to explode. That was so good. Why didn't Dell cook like this before?"

"Yes, honey, it was delicious. Dell cooks that way because Star tells her what to cook," I replied.

"Really? It's Star's doing?" he asked. When I nodded, he said, "I should have let Dad marry her before."

I smiled at him and asked, "How do you feel about Star now? Is her living here what you imagined it would be like?"

"No, Mom, it's way better. I like having Star here. Since she married dad, we eat better food, and the house looks better with all those plants. I always thought she would take Dad away from me, but I see Dad a lot more now," Ned replied.

"I'm glad you like Star. Now you'd better go to sleep; you have school tomorrow," I said as I reached over and kissed his forehead. "Good night, Ned. Love you."

"'Night, Mom. Love you more. Thank you for being my mom," he replied.

Before I fell asleep that night, I thought about what Ned had said about letting his dad marry Star. Were the events that led me to become Ned's mother all arranged before I came here? Ned always said it was Jesus who brought me here. If Ned had accepted Star, would Richard have hired me? There were so many things that could have been different. The more I thought about it, the more I believed that it was God's will for me to be Ned's mom.

10

pring came and brought the rain. They said it was the wettest spring they'd ever had in this area. The rain had forced us to stay indoors, but then, for the first time in weeks, the sun was shining. Richard and Star had taken the boys to school, and I was on my own until I had to pick the boys up at three. I decided to go for a hike; I could walk up the quad trail that led to a little bridge and continued up to a bluff that overlooked the ranch. With a snack and water bottle in my pack, I grabbed my camera and set off. I was going past the barn when I met Tex. When I told him where I was going, he said I could take Brute with me. Brute was his black shepherd. She was an old dog and was very loyal to the person she was with.

"Come on, Brute, let's go explore the trail. Bye, Tex. I'll be back by two," I said as I walked on.

The walk took us past the horse corrals and into the evergreen trees where the trail became steeper. It seemed like I got to the bridge in no time. Coming here with Ned always took longer because we stopped to look at different things that interested him. Like the time he found a small garter snake. He had to pick it up and examine it closely. He had wanted to bring it home, but I told him that the snake would be much happier if it stayed in its home. I didn't want any snake close to me, but, of course, I didn't let him know that.

As I crossed the bridge, I noticed that the water was unusually high; it touched the bottom of the bridge. That did not concern me too much, as we'd had a month of rain. I continued to the bluff and sat on the grass by the edge. From there I had a scenic view of the ranch. To the far left there was a meadow, with a small structure in the middle of it. It looked out of place to have a building so far away from the main ranch. As I took a picture of it with my telescopic lens, I noticed there were horses around the building.

I ate my snack and took a few more pictures, then decided it was time to make my way back home. After giving the last of my sandwich to Brute, I said, "Well, Brute, let's go back." I patted her head, then we were off.

I was just going to step onto the bridge when I heard a loud rumble and felt the ground shake. As I looked up, I saw a massive wall of water and debris coming down toward me. I turned to run back, but the water overtook me. Then, everything went black.

I'm so cold. Why can't I move? It's so hard to breathe.

Darkness.

I feel like there's a heavy weight on my chest. When I try to move, why does pain shoot through my body?

Darkness.

I'm so cold. What is happening?

Darkness.

Someone is picking me up.

Darkness.

Oh, there's some warmth. Did someone say my name? I'm so cold; where did the warmth go?

Darkness.

"Trudy, Trudy, can you hear me?"

Someone is talking to me. Why can't I respond?

"Trudy, you're in the hospital. You're safe. Open your eyes, dear, open your eyes."

I'm trying to respond. Why isn't my body listening? I'm trying and trying. Why is it so hard?

Darkness.

"Mom, Mom! Wake up, Mom!"

Ned is here. Oh, I have to open my eyes to see him. I have to open my eyes. Why can't I open my eyes? I have to go take care of Ned. Oh, my sweet boy, I can't open my eyes.

"Look, Dad, Mom's eyes are moving. Dad, she can hear me. Mom, we are here for you; just rest. We'll be here. Just rest and get better."

Yes, son, I will. I'll open my eyes for you, but not today. Maybe tomorrow. I'm so tired now.

Darkness.

Who is that talking in the darkness? Is he talking to me?

"Trudy darling, can you wake up now? Please wake up, Trudy."

Is that someone squeezing my hand? Why can't I respond?

"Trudy darling, there are a lot of people waiting for you to wake up. Ned is missing his mother. Come on, Trudy, wake up. Open those beautiful eyes. Can you do that for me?"

I'm trying. I'm moving my head from side to side. I'm trying to open my eyes again. Is that a little light I see?

"Oh, good! That's a good girl. Now I know that you're still in there. Trudy, you'll be okay; just sleep now. I'll see you in the morning."

Darkness.

I can hear Ned. What else did I hear? Was that Neil? Why would Neil be here? Oh, where is "here"? Oh yes, I remember, I heard someone say that I'm in the hospital. But why?

"Yes, Ned, I came to see your mother. How are you doing? Are you feeling better?"

Why would Neil ask Ned if he was feeling better? Did something happen to Ned? I have to open my eyes. I have to say Ned's name.

"Mom, Mom! Did you say something. If you can hear me, squeeze my hand."

That's Ned's hand in mine; I have to squeeze his hand. Why can't I move my fingers? Why don't they respond? Oh my! My fingers are tightening around Ned's now.

"Dad, Mom just squeezed my hand. Mom, are you waking up? You've been asleep for two days now. Can you open your eyes?"

I'm trying so hard to open my eyes for Ned. Why can't I move or talk?

"Mom just tried to say something. Mom, just open your eyes."

I try to move my arms, but it's still so hard. What is that pain in my back? It feels like it's on fire. I must tell them. Why is my back getting so hot? I must open my eyes. Oh, there's Ned! I must take his hand and tell him I'm okay. I'm trying to talk. Why aren't the words coming out?

"Oh, Mom, you're awake. Mom is awake, Dad," Ned exclaimed as he saw my eyes opening a little.

At once, Richard and Neil were at my side.

"Trudy, do you know where you are?" Neil asked.

I nodded.

"Are you in pain?"

Again, I nodded.

"I'll get the doctor to give you something for that."

I looked around the room. I was in the hospital, but I couldn't remember why. If they told me why, I couldn't remember.

I cleared my throat and tried to speak. "Wh-wh-why am I h-h-here? N-n-ned, y-y-you o-o-ok-k-kay?"

"Mom, I'm all right now. How are you feeling?" Ned replied and came to sit close to me on my bed.

A nurse came in and injected something into the IV tube in my hand. I could feel the heat in my back fade away and the cobwebs clearing from my head. The nurse sat me up a little.

Ned stayed close to me, holding my hand.

I looked at Richard and asked very slowly and in a hoarse voice, "How did I get here?"

"Trudy, you got caught in a washout. It took us a long time to find you. When Neil finally found you, you were half buried in the creek bed. You are a very lucky lady," Richard said.

I could not believe what he had just told me. *What is a washout? What creek bed? Neil found me?* I had so many questions but was just too weak to ask them, so I lay there, trying to regain my bearings. As the day went on, I became more aware of my surroundings.

When the doctor who initially treated me heard that I was awake, he came to examine me. As he looked over my chart, he said, "It's nice to finally meet you, Miss Rendell. I'm glad to see that you are awake."

He came over and checked my pulse, then he said, "Your vital signs look good, considering what you have been through. We put your right leg in traction; you suffered two fractures in that leg. You also have two cracked ribs; that's why it hurts when you breathe. Based on what Mr. Lance has told me about what happened to you, it's a miracle you did not suffer any head injuries. The nurse tells me you have a sore back. We'll have to take an x-ray to see what is causing you the pain." He made a note on the chart then said goodbye.

While the doctor was with me, Richard, Ned, and Neil went out of my room. When Richard and Ned returned, Ned came to sit by me again.

"Mom, I was so worried about you! When you didn't pick us up from school, I knew something bad had happened. Roger told me that you probably had car trouble and you'd be there any minute. But, Mom, you never came." I could see that it upset Ned just to tell me. He lay down beside me and continued, "Roger called Tex to come get us."

"I'm so sorry I worried you, Ned," I said in a very weak voice and tried to bring him closer to me.

Richard saw that Ned was upset, so he came and put his hand on Ned. He looked at me and said, "Yes, you gave us quite a scare, Trudy. Tex called me and said that you had gone up to the bridge and had not returned, so when I got home, we took the quad and went up there to look for you. When we got close to the bridge, it looked like a giant hand had washed away everything in its path, leaving behind broken trees, gravel, and huge rocks. We didn't even see a sign of the bridge."

"Mom, I got so scared. The bridge was gone, and we couldn't find you. We looked all over for you, and when we didn't find you, I started to cry. I thought that you were buried in all those rocks. Dad picked me up and told me we would not stop looking for you until you were found. Oh, Mom, I'm so thankful that God took care of you and helped Uncle Neil find you," Ned said.

"Yes, we were all very worried," Richard said. "When we didn't find you at the bridge, we returned home, and I called Search and Rescue. In no time at all, a group of people gathered at the ranch, ready to look for you. I also called Neil and asked for his help. It was so slow going because of the broken tree limbs and rocks strewn everywhere. It was a mess. It took us a day and a half to find you. Neil found you a mile from where the bridge had been. We were so relieved and thankful that God had answered our prayers. I don't think we had ever prayed so hard. Star spent the entire night praying for you."

Richard saw I was finding it hard to keep my eyes open, so he said, "Ned, we have to let Trudy get some rest. Come, son, let's go get something to eat."

Ned gave me a soft kiss on the cheek and, as he got off the bed, he said, "Mom, I'm just going to be gone a little while. I'll be back soon."

When I woke up, Richard and Ned were sitting at my bedside. They spent the rest of the day with me. When evening came, Ned was so tired, he fell asleep lying beside me.

"I should go and put him to bed. We'll come see you in the morning," Richard said.

"Where are you staying?" I asked.

"Oh, the hospital has given us a room where out-of-town families can stay. I'll take him and let you get some rest. He's so exhausted from all he went through the last few days," Richard said.

Then, I asked, "Where is Roger?"

"Roger is at home with Tex and Dell. Star is attending a teacher's conference here in the city. She said she'll come visit tomorrow.

Good night, Trudy," Richard replied as he picked up Ned and left for the night.

I was awakened by the night nurse checking my vitals. When I opened my eyes, I saw Richard sitting at my bedside.

"Richard? You're back? Where's Ned?" I asked, confused as to why he would leave Ned alone.

"Trudy, it's me, Neil." He stepped closer to the bed and said, "How are you doing? It's so good to see your pretty eyes. For a while I did not know if you'd make it."

"Neil, I thought you had gone back home. I want to thank you for finding me," I said and then repeated. "Thank you."

He smiled and replied. "Trudy darling, I'm just glad to see that you are doing better."

Something in what he said sounded so familiar, but I could not place it.

He came closer to me and took my hand. "Yes, I found you. I was just about to give up, but something deep inside me told me to keep going. I'm glad I trusted my instincts."

I laughed softly and said, "Me too. Tell me how you came about to find me, Neil. Richard said I was out there for more than a day."

"Are you sure you want to know that now? Why don't you give yourself time to heal?" Neil said.

"No, Neil. I want to know. I'm sorry I've caused so much upheaval in all of your lives," I replied.

"Oh, darling, it's not your fault. You didn't cause that dam to burst," Neil replied but did not say more.

Persistent, I asked again, "Will you tell me? Please?"

He shook his head and said, "Trudy, are you sure you're up to this?"

I nodded.

"Okay, but if you get tired, tell me." I nodded again, so he said, "When I got Richard's call, I dropped what I was doing and went to saddle my horse. Earlier in the day, I had heard some rumbling, but I did not thing much of it. When I got to the creek, I was surprised to see all the damage: the creek bed was filled with loose gravel and broken tree limbs. I spent most of the time looking under piles of branches and behind large rocks. My horse could not walk in that debris, so he followed me on the edge of the rocks. I searched all day and continued until it got dark. Instead of going back home, I camped out for the night, thankful it was not raining. At first light, I set off again. Every hour, Richard would text me to see if I had found you. And every time he did, I would text back no. After searching all day and not finding you, I decided it was time to give up the search. I got on my horse, and as I rode, I noticed something blue half buried in the gravel. When I found that it was a pack, I knew that there was a good chance you would be close by. I walked the creek bed very slowly, looking under everything that could possibly hide you. I rounded a bend and saw the path the water had taken, leaving behind a trail of gravel and debris. It had gone past this tree. All its lower branches were broken off. When I took a closer look, I saw what looked like a rag doll hanging from one of the branches. I could see the arms and torso, but no head or legs. It looked so odd that I didn't think it would ever be you. But it was. The sleeve of your shirt was caught on a broken branch. When I got closer to the tree, I saw that your head was facedown, and your legs were buried in the gravel. I could not believe that it was you."

Neil stopped speaking and looked at me. He took my hand in both of his and brought his head down on them. He stayed that way for a few minutes.

Finally, I asked, "Neil, what is it? Are you all right?"

When he looked at me, I saw that he had tears in his eyes.

He wiped away the tears and said, "Trudy, I thought you were gone. I couldn't find a pulse, and it did not seem like you were breathing. I called your name and started to dig you out, all the time telling you I'd have you out of there right away. As I dug, I heard a growl behind me. I thought a wild animal had claimed you and was now going to attack me for taking his prize. But when I turned, I saw Brute. As I kept digging, I kept talking to you and

Brute. When I had most of your legs dug out, I unhooked your arm from the tree and pulled you free. It was then I heard you moan. Oh, Trudy darling, I can't tell you how happy I was when I heard that moan. I was sorry I'd caused you pain, but you were alive. You were alive."

Again, he stopped. This time he kissed my hand.

"Sorry, darling, I'm getting a little too emotional. It's just that you're the first person I've ever saved," Neil whispered.

I smiled and whispered back, "Thank you for doing that. I'll always be grateful. How did you get me home?"

Neil smiled and said, "Trudy darling, we'll have to continue that story at another time. I'll come see you in the morning. It's late, and the nurse told me not to stay long. Good night, Trudy."

"Good night, Neil. Thank you for coming to see me," I replied. As he stood up, he stooped over me and kissed my forehead.

In the morning, when the nurse was changing my gown, she said with a playful tone in her voice, "I have never seen anyone with your skin color before. I hope there are no purple people eaters around here."

As I looked at my arms, I saw that they were covered with purple and dark-blue bruises. Then, looking down to my legs, I saw that one was wrapped and the other was swollen and had the same purple bruising.

I laughed and said, "Oh, I hope that you can keep them away from me."

She smiled and said, "Trudy, you'll be all right. You know what they say: 'Laughter is the best medicine.'"

A short time later, the doctor was making his rounds. When he saw me, he said, "Miss Rendell, you look much better. When I first saw you, I didn't know if you'd make it. How are you feeling?"

"I'm a little sore, but the painkillers are helping," I replied.

He went over to my wrapped leg and asked, "Do you have any sensation in your legs?"

"Oh, a little; they're tingling. My back hurts the worst," I replied.

The doctor nodded and said, "Trudy, that is a good sign; it means you have feelings in your legs. When you came in, your legs were swollen and blue. I'm glad to see that the circulation in your legs has returned. We set the breaks in your right leg but could not put it in a cast because of the swelling. You have two fractures: one just above your ankle and one in your thigh. Once the swelling goes down, we'll put the cast on. The x-ray we took of your back yesterday, shows that you have a small fracture in your tailbone. It should heal quickly. For now, you'll have to remain lying down."

"Do you know how long it will be before you can put my leg in a cast?" I asked.

"Oh, it could take two weeks, but we'll keep an eye on it. You've come a long way already, Miss Rendell," replied the doctor.

Shortly after the doctor's visit, Richard and Ned arrived. They too were surprised by how much better I looked.

When Ned came to sit beside me, I could see he was a little restless.

I took his hand and said, "It's not that much fun sitting here, is it? I guess you miss your friends at school, huh? How many days have you missed now?"

He looked at me and said, "Yes, Mom, I do miss my friends, but I have to be here for you."

"Yes, I know, but the doctor just told me it will take some time for my leg to heal. You've missed a lot of school already; you can't wait here for me to get better. Besides, your dad must get back to the ranch. How about if you come see me on weekends? I'll be all right; the nurses are taking very good care of me," I replied.

"Mom, I'm not leaving you here alone," Ned said in a very sad voice.

Richard came to stand beside Ned and said, "Trudy is right. You've missed a whole week of school now, and we haven't seen Roger. I have to go help Tex on the ranch. Trudy will not be alone, because Star and Uncle Neil will come visit. We'll be here every weekend."

Ned sat for a while, not saying anything.

I could tell he was trying to decide what he should do.

He turned to look at me and in a soft voice said, "Mom, I want to stay with you," Then, looking at his father, he continued to say, "I'll do what you want, Dad. But we have to come every weekend. Promise, Dad?"

"Yes, son, I promise," Richard replied.

That afternoon, when we said goodbye, I was surprised by how hard it was for me to let him go. I did not want them to go. I think Ned handled it better than I did. After they left, it seemed like the pain grew worse, and I became very scared.

I was watching TV when Star walked into my room.

"Hey there, Trudy, how are you?" she asked.

I did not answer but raised my arms for her to give me a hug.

We hugged for a time, then she said, "Trudy, how are you? Are you in pain?"

"Oh, Star, I'm so glad to see you. I'm a little overwhelmed. I miss having Ned and Richard here. But they have things to do; they can't be here all the time," I cried through my tears.

Star moved a chair close to the bed and took my hand, saying, "Trudy, we are here for you. Do you have any pain?"

"No, not now. The nurse gave me something for it. Star, I'm so scared. I know I'm safe and getting good care, but I feel like I'm in danger. There's a constant humming in my head."

"Trudy, you're still in shock. That feeling will go away in time," Star said, giving me a reassuring smile. Then, she asked, "Was Ned okay with going back home?"

"Oh, he handled it well. Much better than I did," I said. "How was he when he found out I was missing?"

"Oh, that poor little boy was crushed. He wanted to go look for you, but Richard told him he would slow down the search, so he agreed to stay with me. He was so lost. We were both so shocked by the news that we took comfort in each other. When I asked him if he would rock with me, he willingly agreed. As we rocked, I sang him songs that he knew. At first, he sang along, but after a while, he got quiet and fell asleep. I rocked him and prayed to God for your safe return. When Richard returned home, he found both of us sleeping in the chair. When he told me that they hadn't found you and that it would be a miracle if they did, I became very concerned. I stayed up all night praying for you. I asked God to take care of you overnight and lead someone to find you. All the next day we waited for news. Other than asking me to call Richard, Ned did not say anything. He wouldn't eat. He just sat by the window, looking out to see if you were coming. Just before Ned's bedtime, Richard came home and told us that Neil had found you. As soon as Ned heard you had been found, he wanted to go see you. I think he thought Neil would bring you home right away. Then, when Richard told us you were hurt—well, Ned just lost it; that little boy was very upset. Richard held him for a long time. When Ned settled down, Richard promised him that at first light, we would take the quads and go see you. He seemed contented with that," Star recounted.

"Oh, my poor little boy, he shouldn't have had to go through that. It makes me so sad to think I caused him pain. Why did this happen to me?" I said.

Star looked at me and said, "Well, God must have His reasons. God gives and takes away. We can't rely on the gifts; we must rely on Him. He'll work it for the good."

"Yes, but right now, I can't see what good can come out of this," I replied, not understanding what she was trying to tell me.

"Trudy, just surviving this is God's doing. Just believe and trust that He loves you and wants the best for you. Remember the study we had just before this happened? It taught that we are in God's hands and nothing can remove us from Him. Would you like me to pray for you now?" Star said.

I nodded my head, so she bowed her head and prayed for my recovery and Ned's comfort.

I thanked her for praying, then asked, "Was Ned okay with me coming to the hospital?"

When Star shook her head, my heart broke. I asked, "What happened?"

"In the morning we took the quads and rode to the creek. The ambulance was already there. It was impossible for us to cross the creek, so the two EMTs and Richard hiked to where Neil had you. Ned and Roger amused themselves by seeing who could throw rocks the farthest. It took a long time for them to return with you. Ned was the first to spot them carrying you on a stretcher. He was so happy that he would be able to be with you again. Just before the EMT put you in the ambulance, we caught a glimpse of you: your face was as white as snow, and your lips were blue. Fortunately, Richard was holding on to Ned, for the poor boy became so upset. But he got out of Richard's hold, ran up to one of the EMTs, and demanded they let his mother go. Roger reminded him to be good because that's what you would want. When the ambulance left, I saw Ned just standing there, watching it go away. He did not cry or ask where they were taking you. I think he just gave up. It was too hard for him to continue to fight," Star replied. She looked at me and added, "Trudy, this is upsetting you. I've told you too much too soon. I'm sorry."

"Star, I want to know what happened to Ned. Please tell me," I asked.

"Are you sure?" she asked.

When I nodded, she said, "We followed the ambulance to the city. All the time it took to get there, Ned didn't say a word. When we got to the hospital, we were told you had been taken directly to the operating room. Ned was not responding to anything we told him—he just stared out into space—so we asked a doctor to take a look at him. The doctor told us that Ned was in shock and advised that he should be sedated. Ned spent the night in the hospital. In the morning, when Richard took him to see you and you would not wake up, he became quiet again. But this time he listened to what Richard told him. We told Ned that you were badly hurt and needed to rest, that you'd be waking up when you were ready to do so."

"Thank you for telling me, Star. I'm so grateful for all the care you and your family have given me. Thank you for making me feel like I'm a part of this family," I said as big tears rolled down my cheeks.

"Trudy, my dear sister, you are a part of this family. Remember, if it weren't for you, we would not be a family," Star answered.

After Star left, I fell asleep and awoke in a cold sweat.

The nurse was standing over me, telling me to be still.

I looked at her and said, "Why? What did I do?"

"You were very agitated and were trying to get out of bed. Trudy, if you want your leg to heal right, you must keep still. Did you have a bad dream?" she asked.

"I don't remember. It felt like the ground gave way beneath my feet. I'm so cold. Is it cold in here? I'm freezing!" I replied.

"I'll get you a warm blanket. Now you stay put," she instructed.

I nodded.

She returned with a warm blanket, and when she draped it over me, it felt like heaven. I lay still and enjoyed the warmth of the blanket, trying to remember what had made me behave that way. The only thing that came to mind was a feeling of darkness. I must have fallen asleep again, for I woke up with a jolt, causing pain to shoot through me. As I caught my breath, I realized that one of my arms was pressed against my broken ribs. I felt cold again, so I rang my buzzer and asked for another warm blanket. Too afraid to go back to sleep, I laid in bed, waiting for the morning.

Oh, how I wished my mother were here with me. I hadn't thought about her too often recently, but now I longed to have her arms around me again.

In the morning, the sun was shining through the window when I opened my eyes, so I must have fallen back to sleep at some point. Although it was bright in the room, I felt I was surrounded by darkness. All day I felt as if the ground was giving way beneath my feet. I would doze off, only to be jolted awake, which caused me more pain. I laid in bed and wished for Neil to come, but Neil never came.

I was watching TV when Star walked in. She was carrying a big bouquet of bright yellow daffodils.

"Hello, Trudy, how was your day?" she said as she placed the flowers on the table beside my bed.

"Oh my, they are beautiful! Thank you. I'm so glad you came," I said, trying to hold back the tears.

Star came to sit on the edge of the bed and asked, "Trudy, are you all right?"

"Star, I've had a really bad day. I think I'm reliving what happened to me. I have these strange sensations, like the ground is giving way beneath me and I'm falling and I'm not able to breathe. I feel so cold. But the worst of the feelings is this darkness that comes over me. If I go to sleep, I wake up with a jolt, causing pain to shoot through me. I'm getting scared of going to sleep," I said as the tears flowed.

"Trudy, what you've gone through is very traumatic. It's only natural that you would relive it. Remember that you are safe now. I've never experienced anything like what you've gone through, but when bad things happen to me, I try to think about the goodness of God. Have you asked Him to help you?"

I smiled weakly and said, "Oh, Star, I don't think God is with me. I only feel darkness and cold."

Star took my hand and said, "Oh, Trudy, keep on believing, dear. God promises that He will never leave you. He's been with you all along. Remember you're a child of God. Just give yourself time to heal."

"Yes, Star, I'll try. I've asked the nurse for something to help me sleep tonight. Neil was supposed to come see me today, but he never did. Would you know why?" I asked.

"Yes. Richard told me that Neil had an emergency at the ranch. Take heart; Ned and Richard will be coming tomorrow night. I'll stay with you until you go to sleep if you want," Star answered.

"Thank you, Star, I would like that. I'm sorry for being so much trouble. You have been so kind to me," I said, reaching for her hand.

"Oh, my little sister, you are not any trouble. Just keep getting better. Remember, you are not alone; the entire family is praying for you," she said as she held my hand.

During the night, I woke up, feeling like I was choking, like I was caught. As I laid in bed, I now knew why I was struggling with those feelings. I remembered the water washing me away. I tried to swim, but I kept getting hit by rocks and branches. I remember being underwater for a while, thinking I would never take another breath. I laid still, trying to convince myself I was all right but could not stop thinking of that dreadful darkness. Then, a horrifying thought came to mind: What if I'd had Ned with me that day? I couldn't let myself think about that. No, I didn't want to think of this darkness any longer.

I turned my thoughts to the family I had, to my little boy who needed me. Then, I remembered the commitment I had made to Jesus and who I was in Him. The little light I saw when I first came to the Lance family appeared again, but this time it was much bigger—big enough to dispel all the darkness that surrounded me.

In the morning, when I saw the sun shining in my room, I felt that the darkness formerly surrounding me was gone. I felt at peace, like the sun was shining in my heart. The humming in my head was gone.

Richard, Star, Roger, and Ned arrived just as I was finishing supper.

"Mom! Oh, I've been so worried about you. Are you all right?" Ned said as he ran up to my bed.

I took him in my arms and gave him the biggest hug I could manage. "Ned, I'm so happy to see you. I've missed you so much. I'm doing okay. How about you? And you Roger; it's so nice to see you again," I said.

They went on to tell me what they had done and about the new puppy Tex had gotten.

"Tex has a new puppy? But doesn't he have Brute? Neil told me that she was with me when he found me. Was she hurt?" I asked.

"Yes, Mom. Uncle Neil said that she was in bad shape, so he had to put her down. He said that she had protected you until he had found you. You should see this puppy; he's so cute. His name is Ace. He's a husky crossed with a Lab," Roger replied.

"Yes, Mom, the puppy is so cute! He's mostly white, with beige ears. You'd like him," Ned added.

"The new puppy sounds wonderful. It's so sad that Brute did not make it. Tex must be sad he lost her," I said.

"Yes, Mom, that's why he got a new puppy." Ned said. And then, just like any little boy would, he changed the subject and asked, "When will you be coming home, Mom?"

"Well, the doctor told me that as soon as the swelling in my leg goes down, they'll put a cast on it, and then I'll be able to move around a little. I'm not sure when I'll be coming home yet. Maybe in a few weeks," I replied.

Ned stayed with me while the others went to run errands. I enjoyed having Ned with me; I loved how he distracted me from thinking about the situation I was in. When Sunday evening came, and we had to say goodbye, we both had tears in our eyes. I saw how brave Ned was acting, so I took heart and did my best to smile at him as he walked away.

After they left, I opened the bag Star had left on the night table. Right on the very top was my Bible. I took it out without even looking at anything else Star had brought me.

I knew the week I was facing would be a long one. Star had returned home with Richard, so no one was in the city to come to visit me. The sensations I had felt the week before faded away, and I was able to have a peaceful rest every night.

One evening, just before retiring for the night, I was reading my Bible, when Neil walked into my room.

"Hey, darling, how are you doing?" he said as he brought a chair closer to the bed.

For a moment I was speechless, but I quickly recovered and said, "Neil, what a nice surprise. I'm getting a little better each day, I suppose. How are you doing?"

"Oh, things are good, and I hope they stay that way. I've had enough excitement for a while," Neil replied.

I did not know if I should ask for details, so I kept quiet.

After an awkward pause, Neil asked, "Trudy, how are you? Are you remembering what happened to you?"

I gave him a curious look and said, "Have you spoken to Star?"

He shook his head, so I told him about what I had gone through during the past week.

"That's a normal reaction to the trauma you've experienced," he replied.

I smiled and said, "Yes, I know; that's what the doctor has told me."

Again, there was a long pause, so I asked, "Neil, will you tell me how you got me to safety?"

He smiled and said, "You still want to know, after all those things you are feeling?"

I nodded, so he continued, "Okay, but you have to tell me if it upsets you. I think I left off just after I had found you." He took a deep breath and said, "Well, let's see. By the time I dug you out, it had started to rain, so I took out my rain poncho and covered us up with it. I held you in one arm and somehow managed to get on my horse, telling him to find home. If it hadn't been for him, I don't know if I would have found my way back to the shack. It was so dark, and the rain was just pouring down. You just grabbed on to me and held on very tight. When we got back to the shack, I texted Richard to tell him I had found you, but it was too late for the rescue team to come get you. It was decided I'd take care of you until morning came. You were so cold and soaking wet. Your clothes were all torn up, so I dried you off and put one of my T-shirts on you. Your right shoulder was out of joint, so I snapped it back into place, and put a splint on your fractured leg. Every time I moved you, you would moan. I'm sorry for that, Trudy."

I smiled and said, "Neil, I forgive you."

Neil returned the smile and continued with his story. "I didn't know if you would make it through the night. I was very concerned about your legs. They had been buried in the gravel for a long time, so I did not think you had any circulation in them. You were covered with bruises, but you had no visible trauma to your head. I covered you up with blankets and a sleeping bag and tried to warm you up. All night I watched over you; I did not know if you would survive the night. When Richard and the EMTs arrived in the morning, I was so relieved. You had warmed up some, but I knew you were not out of the woods yet. The EMTs bundled you up, then the four of us carried you to the ambulance. We had to walk very slowly because every little bump made you moan."

I looked in his eyes and said, "Neil, thank you for caring for me. I guess Brute was not so lucky. The boys told me you had to put her down."

"Yes. She had internal injuries. Poor dog; she was in bad shape. I just don't know how you made it out without having internal injuries like she did. It's a miracle you're still alive," Neil replied. He took my hand and said, "It feels like I'm responsible for you now. I've never saved anyone who was so close to dying before. When I returned to the shack, I felt so alone. I couldn't get you off my mind; I needed to know how you were doing. I called Tex to come take care of my horses, and I came here to see you. Then, just as you woke up, Tex called me to say that one of the mares was having problems, so I rushed back to the ranch to take care of her. The mare had her foal, and the two are all right now."

"Neil, you don't have to feel responsible for me. You found me; I'm so grateful for that. You don't have to put your life on hold for me. Please don't feel like you have to," I said.

He just sat there, holding my hand, and said, "Trudy, these

feelings just don't turn themselves off. You will always be special to me."

"You are special to me too," I said. Then, I asked, "The boys never said you had returned; when did you?"

"I've been here since the beginning of April. Richard knew I was back. I guess he never told anyone," Neil replied.

"Why were you at that shack? It's so far from the rest of the ranch," I asked.

He smiled and said, "Whenever we bring new horses to the ranch, we always isolate them for a while to make sure they don't have any diseases that could infect the other horses. If they're all okay, I'll bring them to be with the rest of the horses sometime in June. Now Darling, I better be going and let you rest. I'm so glad you're getting better. Good night Trudy."

"Thank you for coming Neil. Good night," I replied.

I looked at him walking out of the room and I wished he would have stayed. When he was close to me, I felt like nothing could hurt me.

II

$\mathcal{M}$y injuries healed quicker than the doctor expected. Before Ned came for his second weekend visit, my broken leg was put in a full leg cast, and I was able to get out of bed. That weekend, when Ned came running into my room and did not see me lying in bed, he came to a sudden stop, looking around the room to see where I was.

When he saw me seated in a chair, he said, "Oh, Mom, there you are. You've got your cast! Does that mean we can take you home now?"

"No, not just yet. I have to do some physical therapy and practice walking on crutches. It might take a week or two," I told him.

"Oh, that's so great! Don't you think so, Dad? Mom is coming home soon!" Ned said, overjoyed by the idea that I'd be returning home.

"Yes, Ned, that is great news," Richard said. "Trudy, how are you feeling?"

"I'm feeling a little better every day. I can't wait to come home," I replied.

Ned and I spent a lovely weekend together. Richard dropped him off each morning and came to pick him up just before supper. The nurse brought me a wheelchair, so Ned and I were able to leave my room and explore the hospital.

Ten days later, I returned to the ranch. Everyone made such a fuss over me, but I felt undeserving of all that attention. Richard rescheduled his work to be home with me when Star was at work. They both were so kind and loving. Neil even made a point to come see me every weekend. It felt so strange to have them care for me. When Ned was not at school, he was my constant companion, at my beck and call.

In late June Neil decided it was time to bring his horses down to be with the other horses. As Neil ate breakfast with us that morning, he reminded Richard that he had a surprise for him.

I still had my full leg cast on, so Richard came to get me with the quad and utility trailer. When I hobbled to the trailer, I saw that Richard had placed a horse blanket on the bottom of it. Once I was comfortable on the trailer, Star and Ned joined me for the ride to the corral. Everyone at the ranch was there to witness the big event and to see what the big surprise would be.

As we waited for the horses to arrive, Ned asked, "Mom, do you know what surprise Uncle Neil has for Dad?"

"No, I don't. My guess is that it has something to do with the horses. We'll know very soon. Look, Ned, there they are now."

We watched as Neil's horses ran past and entered the corral. I noticed that something was different with two of the horses: their gait was different from the other horses. Then, I noticed that the horse Neil was riding had the similar gait. These three horses were jet-black and had long, wavy manes and tails. I loved the way they moved; they were very beautiful.

When all the horses were in the corral and Neil had gotten off his horse, Richard went to talk to him.

I heard Richard say, "Neil, we raise bucking horses, not Tennessee walking horses. Why would you bring these three horses to the ranch? We can't use them in rodeos."

"Whoa, whoa! Richard, just wait until you hear their story. Once you hear it, I think you'll agree that you would have done the same. But first, I promised you a surprise. See the light-brown mare with the big diamond on her head and her colt beside her? She's your surprise. Her dad is a champion bucking horse, and the colt's dad is also a champion. I bought them for you. I think they'll add to your breeding stock," Neil said.

Richard jumped into the corral and walked over to the mare.

Neil followed him.

After carefully examining the mare and the colt, Richard said, "They both look like fine horses. Thanks, Neil. Now, what is the story with the others?"

They both walked to Neil's horse, which was hitched to the corral railing not far from where Ned and I sat.

We listened as Neil recounted the story.

"Do you see the ears on my horse? One is bigger than the other," Neil said.

When Richard nodded, Neil continued, "When he was born—I helped him into the world, by the way—his ear was on the side of his head, like a cow's ear. Although we operated on his ear and moved it to where it should have been, the owner was still upset and wanted to put him down. He did not want to have a genetic defect in his horses, so he wanted the mare to be put down also. I bought them before the owner could sell them for dog food. He would not sell them to me before I agreed to have the animals sterilized. I agreed; I could not let these beautiful horses be put down because of a minor defect. I don't think you would have let that happen either, Richard."

"Neil, you did the right thing. I must admit, they are beautiful," Richard replied.

"Would you like to meet them? The darkest-black one is the mother of my horse and the lighter-black mare. Her name is Bell. She is very gentle; Ned could ride her. The daughter's name is Bella. She still needs a little more training. Come, I'll introduce you to my horse," Neil said as they made their way to the horse. "Richard, meet Rae. He's very gentle, but he will not let anyone ride him except me."

Richard went to the horse, rubbed its nose, and said, "Hi, Rae. So you think I couldn't ride you? I've ridden broncos."

Richard took the reins and put his foot in the stirrup. The minute Richard sat in the saddle, he found himself flying off the back of the horse, landing on his hands and knees. Richard was so surprised, it took him a few seconds to realize what had happened.

Neil ran up to him and said, "Richard, are you all right? I told you he wouldn't let you ride him."

Richard stood up, brushed off the dirt, and said, "Well, I never had a horse do that to me before. Did you teach him to do that?"

Neil chuckled and replied, "No, he's just very loyal to me. I raised him from a colt. After I bought the horses, I had just enough money to rent a stall in this guy's barn. I lived and slept with the colt. Rae thinks he's my brother; he'd follow me right into the house if I let him."

"Neil, like you said, I would have done the same and saved the horses. But this is a bucking-horse ranch; if it gets out that we have gentle horses, we might lose our reputation for having robust horses." Richard patted Neil on the back, then asked, "What about that mare and little colt? We've never had a paint horse before."

"I thought we needed to diversify a little, maybe get into barrel racing. The mare belonged to a young girl who got hurt riding. She was so scared of horses that her father practically gave me the mare. She just gave birth to the colt. See the pattern of white and brown on her shoulder? It looks like a rose, so I named her Rose."

"That's a good idea, Neil; a little variety will benefit the ranch. It's so good to have you back, brother," Richard said, then turned to look at Ned and said, "Ned, would you like to try to ride Bell?"

"Oh, I don't know, Dad. What if she does what Rae did to you?" Ned said.

"No, Ned, she would never do that. She's very gentle. I'll saddle her up if you want to ride. What do you say?" Neil said.

Ned got off the trailer and went to stand beside his father and uncle. He looked up at them and said, "Yes, Uncle Neil. If you say she is gentle, I'd very much like to ride her."

Tex volunteered to saddle the horse. When he returned, Neil helped Ned onto the horse and led her for a short distance.

"Can I ride her without you leading her?" Ned asked.

"Are you sure you want to do this?" Neil asked.

When Ned nodded, Neil gave him the reins.

"Okay, Bell, it's just me and you now," Ned said. "Go."

Bell started walking.

Grinning from ear to ear, Ned looked at me and said, "Look, Mom, Bell is so gentle; she doesn't even make me bounce at all. She's so nice." He patted the horse on the neck and rode past me.

When he returned, I said, "She seems to like having you riding her."

Ned led the mare to the corral and got off the horse.

He returned to sit beside me and said, "Mom, when you get better, we'll be able to go riding. Won't we, Dad?"

"Yes, son, if Trudy wants to. Roger, would you like to ride Bell now?" Richard said.

"Yes, Dad, I'd like that. Uncle Neil, would you like to come for a ride with me?" Roger asked.

Neil agreed to go with him, so he mounted his horse and went for a ride with Roger.

After they left, Richard came close to me and said, "You must be exhausted, Trudy. I'll take you back to the house."

Although being outdoors was very nice, I was tired, so I agreed to go back to the house. The doctor had warned me to take it easy, for if I overdid, it might set back my recovery. That was the last thing I wanted. The sooner I got back to normal, the better for everyone. I did not like being a burden to the family.

By the time school ended, I was well enough to slowly return to the routine I had before the accident. I was so grateful to Richard and Star for taking such good care of me. Summer on the ranch was a very busy time. The horses were loaded on livestock trailers to be transported to the rodeos. Tex and Richard were loading the horses when a horse stepped on Tex's foot, breaking a bone in his foot. Star had been looking forward to spending the summer with Richard, but now he would not be home. Now Richard would have to go with the horses to care for them. Star could have gone with him, but she decided to stay home because she did not think I was well enough to care for the boys' full time. I felt so awful.

At the beginning of summer, Star and I spent long afternoons talking and getting to know each other even better. I was glad to have Star with me, but I felt sure she would have preferred to be with Richard.

One afternoon, after Richard had been gone for a month, I said, "Star, why don't you go join Richard? I'm able to get around on these crutches pretty well now. Go be with Richard."

"Trudy, I don't know if that would be a good idea. It might be too much for you to take on," she replied.

"Star, please don't stay here just because of me. Go be with Richard. I'm good. I have Dell and Neil to help me if needed. Please go," I said.

It took me a week to finally persuade her to go. When she finally agreed to go, it made me very happy. When Richard came to get her, Roger decided to go with them, leaving Ned and me at the ranch. Ned liked to have me all to himself. He always had something for us to do. We'd spent time with Bell and Bella, or we'd invite Trevor and Liz to come over. He would play with Trevor, while I visited with Liz and her twins. On hot days Liz would take us all to the lake. I was never bored with Ned around. But I sure wished that this cast could come off.

Neil now lived in the old house, across the road, but I never felt comfortable in going there. Ned often asked if we could visit Neil, and I always said that we would go see him at another time. But we never did.

Neil would occasionally come to the house for supper, but most of the time he ate with the ranch hands at the bunkhouse. He was in charge of the ranch while Richard was away and Tex nursed his broken foot.

One evening, after Ned had gone to bed, I was rocking on the porch swing when Neil stopped by and asked if he could join me.

"Yes, of course," I replied, happy to be able to talk to him again.

He sat next to me and put his arm around my shoulders.

"That feels so nice," I said.

"What's so nice?" Neil asked, giving me a big smile.

"This—you having your arm around my shoulders—seems oddly familiar," I replied.

Neil smiled again, tightened his hand on my shoulder, and said, "Well, darling, you might be remembering the night I rescued you. There is one thing I never told anyone."

"Oh, really, and what is that?" I asked.

He smiled again and said, "You were frozen. I had to warm you up, and the only way I could do that was to cuddle up with you in the sleeping bag. You were so cold, you just stole all the warmth I had. You practically turned me into an ice cube."

I had to laugh when I imagined Neil as an ice cube. Then, realizing what he had just told me, I said, "You mean we slept together?"

"It was more like you shivered, and I worried," Neil replied, giving my shoulder another squeeze.

We swung in silence for a while.

Then, Neil asked, "How are you feeling, Trudy?"

"I'm better, Neil. The doctor said that my leg is healing well, and he thinks the cast should be off by the end of the month. Again, Neil, I thank you for all you have done for me; for rescuing me and coming to visit me. You're so kind," I said.

"You're welcome, Trudy. It was great to talk to you again. Take it easy. I'd better be going. I've got to get an early start tomorrow. Good night, Trudy," he said as he got off the swing.

"Good night, Neil. See you tomorrow," I replied.

As I watched him walk away, I realized that he was my hero. Then, I remembered how good it felt when he was close to me.

Could I be falling in love with Neil? I wonder if he feels the same about me, I thought.

I pushed the thoughts away and decided to go to bed.

Ned had never voiced any interest in the ranch to me prior to that summer, but now Neil's horses were a constant topic of conversation. One day, while we were in the barn, taking care of Bell and Bella—brushing them and feeding them special treats—Ned asked Neil if he could ride Bella. Neil and Roger had been training Bella, but before he would let Ned ride her, Neil decided to ride her to see how she would do. He rode her around the corral a few times. Bella was a magnificent horse. She held her head and tail up high. Her gait was so smooth that the rider did not bounce at all.

Neil patted her neck and as he got off, said, "I think you're showing off."

He helped Ned onto Bella then adjusted the stirrups to fit Ned's legs. Once done Ned rode around the corral the way Neil had. I could tell that Bella was now more subdued. She knew that Ned was not her normal rider.

When Ned dismounted, he said, "Now that I can ride Bella, Mom, you can ride Bell, and we could go for a ride. That would be so great, Mom, don't you think?"

"You want me to ride a horse? I've never ridden before," I said, uneasy even at the thought of it.

"Uncle Neil will teach you, just like he taught me. Right, Uncle Neil? You'll teach Mom to ride, won't you?" Ned said.

"Ned, slow down," Neil said. "Trudy is just recovering from a big injury; she might not want to risk getting hurt again."

"No, it's not that. When I was a little girl, I always loved horses, but they scared me because they were so big. I know Bell is very gentle. If you are willing to teach me, Neil, I would like to learn to ride," I replied.

"You would, Mom? Oh good," Ned said, smiling from ear to ear.

"Trudy, it will be my pleasure to teach you, but we'll go slow. I don't want you to get hurt," Neil said.

Once my cast was off, my riding lessons started. On the first day of my lessons, as I was walking by Rae's paddock, he let out a loud neigh.

Neil was close by and heard it. He came to the door of the paddock and said, "I'm sorry, Rae, I've never introduced you to Trudy."

The horse nodded, put his head over the half door, and tried to smell me.

"Put out your hand for him to smell it. He knows you're the one he saved," Neil said.

I held my hand by Rae's nose. After he had smelled it, I patted him, saying, "Thank you for being there, Rae, and finding your way home."

The horse again nodded his head and gave a low neigh.

"Does he really know it was me?" I asked.

"Oh, he knows it was you. He thinks you're special. He might even let you ride him," Neil replied.

"Really, how do you know this?" I asked.

Neil shrugged his shoulders and said, "I know my horse."

It did not take long for me to get comfortable riding Bell. She was such a great horse. Once I was comfortable on the horse, the three of us would go for long rides together: Neil riding Rae, Ned riding Bella, and me riding Bell. It was such a wonderful time. I noticed that neither Neil nor Ned ever picked the path leading to the creek that had just about claimed my life.

12

At the beginning of September, the doctor gave me a clean bill of health, but I still walked with a slight limp. Star and Roger returned home, while Richard stayed to finish the rodeo season. Ned and Roger returned to school, and Star returned to work, leaving me with time to myself. The afternoons when the boys were at school, I often went to see the horses. I loved to talk to them, especially Rae. He would respond as if he knew what I was saying to him.

Neil came in the barn one afternoon when I was talking to his horse. He came over to the paddock and said, "Rae, don't let a pretty girl turn your head. Trudy could be spoken for."

The horse neighed and nodded his head.

"Whatever do you mean by that?" I asked.

Neil looked me in the eye, started to say something, but stopped himself. He turned to the horse and said, "Would you like to go for a ride, Trudy? It's a nice afternoon."

"Yes, that's a wonderful idea, but I have to be back in time to go get the boys from school," I replied.

Neil saddled up the horses, and we set out.

As we rode, Neil said, "Let's go ride by my house. I want to show you something."

I told him to lead the way.

After a short time, we passed the old house and went down the road a way. When we turned down a lane I hadn't noticed before, I was surprised to see a bulldozer pushing down trees.

"Why are you clearing the trees?" I asked.

He got off his horse and came to help me off mine.

"This is the start of the veterinary clinic and animal hospital I'm building," Neil replied. "I just approved the final plans and hope to have it built by Christmas. The general contractor is supposed to be here. Let's go see if we can find him."

We walked our horses around the clearing and found the contractor sitting on a stump, watching the dozer work.

Neil went to talk to him, while I stayed with the horses a short distance away.

As we made our way back to the barn, Neil said, "I don't think I'll have very many afternoons like this one very often now. This project will take all of my time."

"Yes, it's a big undertaking. How big will the building be?" I asked.

"The building will house the clinic and the hospital in the front, and a big riding arena in the back. I want to build the arena so that I can train horses year-round. The plan calls for two examination rooms and an area where I can do surgeries. There'll also be paddocks and stalls for the bigger animals, outside the building," Neil replied.

When we got back to the barn, Neil helped me off the horse. As we walked the horses to the corral, Rae pushed Neil closer to me.

At first, Neil ignored him, but after the third time, Neil turned and said to the horse, "Will you stop doing that? Stop bossing me around. It's not any of your business."

Neil then turned to me and said, "Sometimes he thinks he's smarter than I am."

I laughed and said, "You talk to him like he was a person. Does he know what you're telling him?"

"Yes, I think he does. Ever since I got him, he's put his nose in my affairs. He can be very pushy if he doesn't get what he wants," Neil replied. He turned to the horse, patted his nose, and said, "Don't you, boy?"

Neil went to unsaddle the horses, and I returned to the house just in time to go get the boys.

Richard returned home just in time for Roger's birthday.

While we were eating birthday cake, Ned said, "Mom, when is your birthday? You've been here for a year now, and we never celebrated your birthday."

"Ned's right. Trudy came here just after my birthday last year," Roger said.

Everyone looked at me, making me very uncomfortable.

"Well, Trudy, are you going to tell us?" Neil asked.

I smiled reluctantly and said, "My birthday is April 14."

Neil looked at me in disbelief and said, "That's the day I rescued you."

I nodded as a cold shiver went down my back.

"Trudy, we have to celebrate having you here for a year. Next Friday, when everyone is here, we'll have a celebration," Richard said but made no mention of my birthday.

As the months went by, Neil often came for supper very unhappy. He would complain that the contractor was not doing his job and that he had to be consistently on his case. I think Neil was getting impatient because he wanted to get his business started, and every little delay upset him. It surprised me to see Neil acting that way; he was always patient and in a happy mood whenever he was with me.

As Neil had said, he was very busy with his project, I only saw him when he came for supper. He mostly spoke to Richard about the clinic and hospital. We rarely had a private conversation. In the middle of November Neil invited everyone for a tour of the clinic and hospital. I was surprised to see that the building was near completion. As we entered the building, Neil showed us where the examination rooms and the operating room would be. Then, going through a door at the back of the building, we entered the big arena.

"Oh, this is so big, Uncle Neil! We would be able to ride the horses in here," Ned commented.

"Yes, Ned, that's why I built it. When it's too cold to exercise the horses outside, we can ride them in here," Neil replied.

Neil continued the tour, showing us the upstairs, where his office would be and where supplies would be stored.

Winter soon set in, and Christmas was only a month away. Neil and I were sitting on the La-Z-Boys in the living room, enjoying some quiet time. Richard and Star had gone out for the evening, and the boys were in bed.

We were just making small talk, when I said, "I can't believe how fast the past year has gone by. So many things have changed in my life. You never know what to expect in this life, do you?"

"You are sure philosophical tonight," Neil replied. "But I know what you mean. I spent last Christmas with my horses. They don't give very pleasant presents. This Christmas is so much better; I'm back with the family I love."

"Yes, it would be. Didn't you have any friends you could have spent Christmas with?" I asked.

"Oh, I had friends, but none of them invited me to join them. I didn't want to impose, so I spent Christmas with the horses," Neil replied.

We were quiet for a while, then I said, "Well, you're here this year, and I'm glad you are. If not for you, I wouldn't be here. I will be grateful to you forever."

"Trudy, I'm glad I found you when I did. You are a very lucky lady," Neil said.

"I don't think it was luck that you found me. I think God had His hand in it," I replied.

Neil shook his head and said, "Well, it could be. I don't know much about how God works. But, yes, it was a miracle that I found you when I did."

I smiled at him.

He returned the smile, then asked, "Trudy, I've been wondering if you would be my receptionist. It would be only until I can hire someone. I want to start with someone I can trust."

"Well, I don't know. My first responsibility must be to the boys. Richard hired me to be their nanny."

"Yes, of course. I'm talking about when the boys are at school. Would you?"

"Have you spoken to Richard about this? He might not want me to take extra work."

"Okay, I'll talk to Richard. If he agrees, would you do it?"

"Yes, Neil, if Richard agrees, I'll do it."

"Good. That will help me out a lot. I'm planning to hire a receptionist once we're open full time. Thank you, Trudy. You're the very first person I've ever hired." Neil stretched and added, "Well, it's getting late. See you tomorrow, Trudy. Good night."

Time flew, and the veterinary clinic and animal hospital was scheduled to open in a week. All was ready, except for setting up the equipment Neil would need in the operating room.

Ned and I organized the reception area and stocked up the pet supplies in the little store just to the side of the reception desk. All the time we worked, Ned talked, telling me about what he was doing at school and how much he loved riding Bella. We covered a lot of subjects during the time we worked.

Neil bought a computer and a program to keep track of the clinic records. The day the IT person came to show him how to run the program, Neil asked me to come so that I would know how it worked.

After the IT person left, Neil stood there, looking at the computer, shaking his head. He looked at me and said, "You'll have to take care of this computer business, Trudy. I'm no good with computers."

"I'll gladly do that, Neil. I took a computer course in college and if I need help, I'm sure I could call tech support," I answered.

When the building was all finished, Neil held an open house. It was well attended, most of the people in the area came to see the new veterinary clinic and animal hospital. The ranchers were impressed with the facility and pleased to have a veterinarian in the area.

As I looked over the crowd, I saw a lady with blonde hair and perfect makeup. She made her way to Neil and said something to him. Neil gave her a polite smile and quickly moved away from her.

Later, I was by the refreshment table when Neil came to get a drink.

I smiled and said, "Looks like you have a fan."

"Yes, she seems to be there every time I turn around. She told me her name is Lisa. She must be new to this area; I've never seen her before," Neil said, then asked, "How are you doing? It's been a long day. I don't want you to overdo."

"I'm all right. I already have two appointments for you tomorrow. Easy ones: a guy with a new puppy, who says the pup needs his shots; and this Lisa, who has a kitten she wants you to look at," I replied.

The clinic opened the following afternoon. Neil's first client was Lisa, who arrived with her small kitten. As soon as she saw Neil step into the reception area, I could tell that her only interest was Neil, for she totally forgot she even had the kitten with her.

"Hi, Dr. Neil! Remember me? I'm Lisa. We met yesterday at the open house. I hope we can get to know each other. I'm having a party tonight; I hope you can come," Lisa said as she and Neil made their way to the examination room, leaving the door open.

"How old is this kitten? It's way too young to have been taken away from its mother," I heard Neil say.

Then, I heard Lisa say, "Do you think you can make it to my party, Dr. Neil?"

"No, Lisa, I'm afraid I can't make it. Now, I asked you about the kitten. It's so little; I think you should bring it back to its mother," Neil said.

"Oh, that's too bad; we would have so much fun," Lisa replied.

Neil returned to the reception desk and handed me the kitten. He turned to Lisa and said, "If you want this kitten to live, take it back to its mother. Goodbye, Lisa."

"Okay, Dr. Neil. See you soon," Lisa replied.

She turned to walk out, but before she got to the door, I said, "Excuse me, miss, aren't you forgetting something?"

She looked at me with an inquiring expression, but when she saw I was holding the kitten, she came to get it.

With only two days before Christmas, Neil and the boys went out to get the Christmas tree.

When they returned, Ned came to find me and when he did, he exclaimed, "Mom, Uncle Neil let me drive the snowmobile, and I didn't even get it stuck. Roger said I would, but I didn't." He took my hand and continued, "Oh, Mom, come see the tree. Uncle Neil got a really big one. I think it's bigger than the one we had last year."

Ned led me to the living room, where Roger and Neil were getting ready to stand the tree. Like Ned had said, it was big and very bushy.

When Neil saw me, he asked, "What do you think? Too big?"

"It is big, but you got it through the door. Now all we have to do is decorate it," I answered.

When Richard and Star stepped into the room, they were very surprised that Neil had gotten the tree inside the house and remarked that we would have to go get more decorations.

When Neil heard that, he said, "Well, we could make some. Star, would you have any colored cardboard paper? We can make a paper chain."

Once we had all the supplies we needed to make the decorations, Ned and I started to cut the cardboard into strips, while Roger and Neil stapled them in alternating red and green, interlocking rings. As we made the chain, Richard and Star put on the lights and the garland. When we finished making the chain, it was long enough to encircle the tree three times. When all the other decorations were on the tree, Neil helped Ned placed the star on the top of the tree. Once that was done, we all stepped back to admire our creative endeavor. We all agreed that the tree looked terrific.

This was my second Christmas with my new family. So many

things had happened since last Christmas. As I went to sleep that night, I gave thanks to God for bringing me here and for His care during that awful accident. This Christmas was so much more special than the last; I now knew my Lord Jesus, and I was Ned's mother.

Like last Christmas, Ned was in a Christmas pageant at church and was very excited to have Uncle Neil come to church with us. When we got there, it surprised me how comfortable Neil was to be there and how well known he was. It made me wonder why Neil had never attended church with us before.

On Christmas Day, Neil dressed as Santa and handed out the gifts. I could tell he loved playing the part. Later when everyone was opening their gifts, I noticed Neil was not opening his gifts but was watching us as we did.

Ned saw that too and said, "Uncle Neil, why aren't you opening your gifts? Here, this one is from Mom."

Neil took the gift and said, "Well, it must be a very special gift. I'd better open it."

I was a little anxious to see what his reaction to the gift would be.

When he lifted the gold chain with the horse pendant from its box, he said, "This is very unexpected. I've never had a neck chain before, but it's from you, darling, so I'll wear it. Thank you."

The look he gave me made me blush, and I'm sure everyone in the room noticed it.

As I was helping Star in the kitchen that afternoon, she said, "I've noticed that Neil likes to tease you a little. How do you feel about that?"

I looked at her and replied, "Oh, I don't mind when it's just the two of us, but with all the family there, it can get a little embarrassing."

She smiled and said, "I think he likes you."

"Oh, you think so? He told me he feels responsible for me, but I don't think he's too serious. After all, he's married," I replied.

Star nodded and said, "Yes, but he could get an easy divorce."

I did not want to go on with this subject, so I said, "Will you be setting the table the same way you did last year?"

Star gave me a knowing look and said, "Yes, my dear sister."

That evening, as the family sat down to enjoy a delicious Christmas meal, we all joined hands for the blessing. Richard gave thanks for everyone sitting at the table. He especially thanked God for bringing Neil home and for protecting me and keeping me with them.

The day after Christmas I asked Ned, "What would you like to do for your birthday this year?"

"You know Mom, I really wish I could have a riding party, at Uncle Neil's arena. Do you think he would let us?" Ned replied.

"I'll ask him, I don't think he would say no," I replied.

The day before the big day, with Richard's and Neil's helped we decorated the arena with big balloons and streamers. Because this was a riding party, Ned only invited kids who were accustomed to being around horses and were able to ride. It was all arranged, on New Year's Day we celebrated Ned's seventh birthday.

All the eight boys Ned had invited to the party came. After what Ned must have told them, they were all very curious to see Neil's horses. Bell and Bella patiently gave everyone rides. After the kids had a few rides around the arena, Richard and Star served a lunch of homemade pizza.

I brought out the cake, and when Ned saw it was a strawberry shortcake, he was very surprised.

When the party ended and all our guests had gone, Ned came to me and said, "That was the best party ever. Thank you, Mom."

"You're welcome. Have you thanked the horses? I think Bell and Bella were happy to see the day come to an end. They must have gone around the arena a hundred times," I said, giving him a big hug.

"Yes, Mom, I did. I even gave them a piece of birthday cake. They liked it," he replied with the biggest grin on his face.

With the holidays over, Neil reopened the clinic. As the month of January went by, he became so busy, he couldn't handle it on his own. Late one afternoon, after he had been gone all day on an emergency call, he returned and saw all the missed appointments.

"I think I'm going to have to hire an assistant to help me," Neil said. "Someone who can take care of the small animals while I'm away taking care of the big ones. I'll call my old school to see if they know of someone."

"We could hire a receptionist too. That way, we could stay open for more hours, and it would give me more time to look after the books," I added.

"That's a good idea. You were not supposed to be spending so much time here. Richard has been so good letting you work for me," Neil said. "I don't think Ned minds, though; he likes helping around here."

Neil placed an ad for a receptionist in the local newspaper and on social media. He called his school and asked them to help him find him an assistant.

A week later, Neil informed me that he had received a response to the ad. With a big smile on his face he added, "Trudy, you'll never guess who applied."

"Who?" I asked.

Neil wordlessly handed me the résumé he had received.

My eyes just about came out of my head when I saw who it was: Lisa, the lady with the kitten.

"Oh, you can't be thinking of hiring her! Are you?" I asked.

He smiled and said, "It's the only response we've received. She says she can type and answer phones. She also says that she can make coffee and would get me some. You never do that."

I turned and went back to the work I had been doing.

Neil followed me to the office and said, "If we don't get any more responses, we might have to hire her."

"Really? You can't be serious! She'd get you a lot more than coffee," I said.

I could not see myself working with Lisa, but then I thought that maybe I was being too critical.

A month passed, and no one else responded to either ad. Neil was seriously considering calling Lisa for an interview. Then, late one afternoon, there was a call from a young-sounding woman asking if the assistant position was still available.

I quickly ran to find Neil and gave him the phone.

When he got off the phone, I asked, "Well, how did it go? Tell me what she said. Is she interested? Neil, please say something."

He handed me the phone and said, "Well, she sounds very young. I don't know if she would be what we want. Her name is Wendy. She said she'll be in town next Monday and is looking forward to our meeting. I'm going to meet with her there, would you like to come with me?"

"You want me to come to the interview?" I asked, surprised that he would include me.

"Trudy, you'll have to work with her too. Even if you didn't, I value your opinion," Neil replied.

On Monday morning Neil and I were sitting in the restaurant at the appointed time when a young couple walked in.

The young lady came to our table and said, "We're looking for Dr. Lance."

Neil stood up and said, "I'm Neil Lance. You must be Wendy." When she nodded, Neil extended his hand and said, "Pleased to meet you, Wendy."

Wendy shook Neil's hand, then turned to the guy she was with and said, "Dr. Lance, this is my boyfriend, Grant."

Neil shook Grant's hand, then invited them to sit.

Once they were seated, Neil introduced me and then said, "We were about to order. Would you like something to eat?"

"No thank you. I'm just too nervous to eat. I'm so excited to be here. I'm from the city and have always dreamed of living in the country. It's so pretty here, with the fresh air and the wide-open spaces. I just love it!" Wendy exclaimed.

I liked her enthusiasm.

She told us about her education and her work experience.

Neil asked her a series of questions, and with each answer, I saw his smile get wider.

"Wendy, I need help at my clinic. I'd like to offer you the position. When can you start?" Neil said.

"Dr. Lance, there is just one thing. Grant is looking for work, and if he can't find a job here, I won't be able to take the assistant position. Would you know of someone who is hiring?" Wendy said.

When I heard her response, my heart sank. I liked Wendy.

Neil must have felt the same, for he asked, "Grant, what kind of work are you looking for?"

"I'm a heavy-duty mechanic, but I'm willing to learn new things. I'm willing to do just about anything," Grant answered.

"He's like MacGyver. He can fix anything! If he can't, he'll find a way to get it fixed. He's really good at what he does," Wendy boasted.

Neil smiled at her and said, "Let me talk to my brother; he might have an opening on the ranch. I'll let you know."

That evening as we were finishing supper, Neil said, "Richard, I think we have an assistant for the clinic. There is just one thing. She has a boyfriend who needs work. He says he's willing to do just about anything. Would you agree to meet with him?"

"I'm always looking for good ranch hands. Someone who can work on his own. Sure, I'll talk with him," Richard replied.

"Thanks for your help, Richard, I'll call Wendy and asked her if she and Grant could come to the ranch in the morning," Neil said.

I was just returning from driving the boys to school when I met a motorbike with two people on it. I was opening the gate when they stopped beside my car. They got off the bike and took off their helmets. I was very relieved when I saw that it was Wendy and Grant.

I greeted them and instructed them to follow me in. After closing the gate, I led them to the house.

When they got to the house and got off the bike, Wendy looked around and said, "I can't believe I'm on a real-live ranch. Grant, look, there's cows just over there. I never knew a place like this really existed."

I smiled at her, remembering my reaction when I first arrived here. Just as I was going to invite them into the house, Neil and Richard met us on the porch.

"Oh, you made it. I was wondering if my directions were clear enough for you to follow," Neil said when he saw them. He turned to Richard and said, "Richard, meet Grant and Wendy."

Richard shook hands with them and invited them for a tour of the ranch.

I was working at the clinic, when they all came walking in.

As they entered, I heard Wendy say, "I still can't believe I'm on an actual ranch! It's so beautiful here. Mr. Lance, you are so fortunate to live here. Thank you for hiring Grant."

As they approached the office, she turned to Neil and said, "Dr. Lance, thank you for hiring me, it's everything I have always dreamed of."

After Neil showed Wendy and Grant around the clinic and hospital, Grant went with Richard, while Wendy stayed at the clinic.

As we stood around the reception desk, Neil said, "Trudy, would you show Wendy our computer system?" He turned to Wendy and said, "Trudy knows more about the program than I do. I'll leave you with her. I have a few calls I have to make."

Before he could leave, I asked, "Neil, when will Wendy be starting? Do I start making appointments for her?"

"Trudy, I think you can start right away. I'm eager to get started," Wendy replied.

Neil looked at me and said, "You heard the lady."

I explained the computer program to Wendy and showed her where the files for the clients were kept. It wasn't long before she knew her way around the clinic.

We set up a routine. Wendy would open the clinic and man the phones until I came in after taking the boys to school. After I got there, Neil would do the surgeries, with Wendy assisting him. Appointments were scheduled for the afternoons. Everything was working well, except for one thing: I had to go get the boys from school every afternoon and often left unfinished work on my desk. This was stressing me out. So, one afternoon, I said, "Neil, we have to hire a receptionist. It's not good to have the boys wait for me to get off work every day."

"I could put another ad in the paper. Lisa would probably see it and wonder why I never hired her," Neil replied.

"Yes, I know. Lisa comes in every other day, asking to see you. I keep telling her you're busy. She'll wait for a while, then leaves. I think she's stalking you," I said.

Wendy had been listening to us and said, "I know who we could hire for the job."

"Who? You know someone?" I asked.

"Yes. Why not hire Grant for the hours Trudy has to be away?" she suggested.

"Grant would be willing to do that?" I asked.

Wendy smiled and said, "Grant is able to do anything. I'll ask him, if you want."

Neil was on board with having Grant fill in for me.

The next morning when I arrived at the clinic, Grant was sitting in the receptionist chair. With a big smile on his face he greeted me and said, "Trudy, Wendy tells me you need help. I'm your man. Just show me what you want me to do."

"You're sure you want to do this? Maybe Tex has something for you to do," I said.

"No. I passed it by him, and he said if Neil needs help, that's what I should do. Besides, it's only for a few hours a day," Grant replied.

Grant was very nice, and I found him to be a quick learner.

I was showing Grant our filing system when Lisa came in. As soon as she saw Grant, she said, "I'm here to see Dr. Neil."

Grant asked her if she had an appointment.

"No, but I usually see him without one. He'll see me; just tell him I'm here," Lisa replied.

"Dr. Neil is not here at the moment, but we have an opening for this afternoon, I could book you in," Grant said.

"No, it's okay. Maybe I could talk to you about my kitten. Are you a doctor?" she asked.

Grant smiled and said, "No, I'm not a doctor; I'm a heavy-duty mechanic. I fix machinery, not animals. If you want, I could show you how I fixed the baler yesterday. I could have used your little fingers to get the bolt I dropped."

Lisa gave him a horrified look and said, "I've got to be going. Bye." She couldn't get out the door fast enough.

With Grant coming to relieve me at the clinic, I was able to relax and enjoy the time I had with the boys. We would take Bell and Bella to the arena and ride them. At first, Tex would come with us to saddle the horses, but once I learned how to do that, we were on our own. The boys would put the horses through their paces, just like Neil had shown them to do. I so enjoyed watching Bell and Bella. It seemed like they were competing, but in a loving way. Bella was the show-off; she would put her head and tail higher than Bell did. Then, Bella would prance around the arena, lifting her feet high as she walked. When Neil had time, he would come to watch. I enjoyed those times immensely.

In early spring 4-H Canada would start again, and Roger needed a project. He decided to ask Neil if he could train Rose's colt. Neil eagerly agreed; he liked when the boys showed interest in his horses. Now we brought three horses to the arena. Roger would work with Bud, Rose's colt. When Roger told us what he had named the colt, we all thought it was an appropriate name. With Roger working with the colt, I was able to ride Bell. I soon found that I enjoyed riding, and I looked forward to it every day.

The months went by, and winter turned into spring. On the morning of my birthday Ned reminded everyone what day it was. It was a bittersweet day for us all as we recalled the accident. The day was just like any other day, until supper time. When we got to the house, I found that Dell had made a special meal, and there was a big chocolate birthday cake sitting on the counter. I went to change for supper, and when I returned, the house was full of people. I found out later that Ned had invited Liz's family and all the people who worked on the ranch to attend my birthday party.

While we were eating supper, Richard said, "Trudy, we all want to wish you a happy birthday. This party was all Ned's doing. He had help, but he chose the food and the flavor of the cake." Raising his glass, which was filled with raspberry juice—also Ned's choice—he said, "To Trudy, our nanny, we thank you for all you do around here. Happy birthday, dear."

"Dad, Trudy is not just our nanny; she is my mother!" Ned exclaimed.

"Of course, Ned. To our nanny and Ned's mother," Richard toasted again. Everyone raised their glasses and wished me well.

Dell served the delicious supper of roast beef she had prepared and once we had finished eating, Ned brought the cake to the table. As Neil helped him light the candles he said, "I don't know how old you are mom, so I put all the candles that were in the box." I laughed and said, "That's alright Ned, thank you for doing that." After I blew out the candles, Neil cut out a slice and as he handed it to me, he winked and said, "There you go birthday girl, enjoy!"

I thanked him, hoping no one had seen the wink.

When everyone had finished eating their cake, Ned turned to me and said, "I'll be right back, Mom." Then, turning toward his brother, he said, "Roger, will you help me?"

The boys went out of the dining room, returning with a big box and set it down beside me.

Looking very pleased, Roger looked at me and said, "Trudy, this is from all of us."

When I opened the box, I found a complete riding outfit: high-top boots, beige riding pants, a black leather jacket, and a riding helmet.

"This is such a surprise. Thank you," I said, feeling tears coming to my eyes.

"Mom, you should go put it on and see if it fits," Ned said. "The lady at the store said you could return it if it didn't. Right, Miss Star?"

"Yes, dear, she did," Star replied, smiling broadly at Ned. "I went with Ned to get the outfit, Trudy, but he's the one who picked it out."

Star later told me that Ned had asked her to take him shopping so that he could get me the outfit.

I went to change, and to my surprise, everything fit perfectly.

When I returned to the dining room, Ned looked at me and said, "You will look so pretty wearing that riding Bell, Mom. Won't she, Uncle Neil?"

I looked at Neil and saw he had the biggest smile on his face. He winked at me and said, "Yes, Ned, your mother is very pretty."

As I continued to look at Neil, I could feel my face getting red. Other than my mom, no one but Neil had ever said I was pretty. Coming from him, it made me blush even more.

13

On a beautiful June morning, while we were finishing our coffee before setting off to work, Tex came in with a special-delivery letter for Neil. When he showed me the envelope, I saw that the return address read, "Matthew Hill, Attorney-at-Law."

As he opened the envelope, Neil said, "I wonder what this is about. Maybe I'm being sued." He took the letter out of the envelope and started to read it. As he read, I saw his face go completely white.

Richard must have noticed Neil go pale, because he asked, "Neil, what is it? You look like you've just seen a ghost."

"I think I have," he replied as he handed the letter to Richard.

"Well, I'll be. I can't believe it," Richard said, as he read the letter and handed it back to Neil.

Star seemed concerned and said, "Richard, is something wrong? What does the letter say?"

"It seems that I'm the father of four kids. It's a letter from my estranged wife's lawyer. It says that she died in childbirth and left me with four kids," Neil said in a stunned voice.

"Oh, that has to be a hoax. How can you be the father of four kids when you haven't seen your wife in seven years?" I asked.

"Oh, I don't think it's a hoax, Trudy. The letter has many details that only this family would know about. No, I think it's legit. It says my name is on the children's birth certificates, and since we were never divorced, I'm their legal father—even if I'm not their biological one. The lawyer wants me to make arrangements to come get the children, or they will be up for adoption," Neil replied. He reread the letter, then said, "What in the world am I going to do with four kids?"

Everyone was quiet for a while until Richard said, "Jill was Amanda's sister, so these kids are Roger and Ned's first cousins. They're part of this family. Neil, they have to come here; they have no one else."

"Does the letter say how old the children are?" Star asked.

"Let's see," Neil said, scanning the letter. "The twin boys are six, then there's a three-year-old girl, and the newborn, also a girl." Looking at Richard, Neil said, "Will you help me with this, Richard? I don't think I can take care of four kids on my own."

"Neil, this is a family. We take care of our own. Star, what do you say?" Richard said.

"Neil, I'll do what needs to be done," Star replied.

Neil nodded his thanks, then looked at me and said, "Trudy, are you willing to help me also?"

"You have to ask? Neil, you know I'll help," I said.

"Okay, I'll call this lawyer and see how he wants us to proceed," Neil said.

After calling the lawyer and making an appointment to meet with him, Neil said, "Richard, would you come with me to see the lawyer? I have an appointment for tomorrow afternoon."

When Richard agreed, I saw a look of relief on Neil's face.

That evening, after the boys were in bed, I went to sit on the porch swing. It had been a full year since my accident, and my injuries had fully healed. It felt good to be able to relax and admire the scenery. A little later, I was surprised when Neil came to join me.

As he sat down beside me, Neil said, "What a day! This morning, when I got up, for all intents and purposes, I was a single guy without a care in the world. Now I'm a father of four. It sure has been a surprising turn of events."

"Yes, every day is special. I take every day as a blessing now," I replied.

"Yes, after what happened to you, I imagine every day would be special. But what I meant was that the lawyer's letter has changed my life completely. I don't have a wife now, but I have four kids. You know, after Jill left, I never really missed her. I was kind of relieved she was gone. We were always fighting about one thing or another. I never had any peace living with her. Now that I know she's really gone, I regret I didn't do more to find out where she was. She was my first love. I did love her, but I don't know if she ever loved me. I'm sorry, Trudy, I didn't mean to go on like this," Neil said in a remorseful voice.

I touched his hand but could not think of anything to say.

We sat in silence for a while, then Neil said, "Tomorrow is going to be a big day. I'd better get some sleep."

Neil turned toward me and brought me close to him. I thought it was for a hug, but then, very unexpectedly, he kissed me.

He then quickly got up and said, "Good night, darling. I'll see you in the morning."

I sat there stunned, watching him walk away.

The next morning, when I went for breakfast, I found Star sitting all alone, having a cup of coffee.

"Good morning, Star. Where's Richard?" I asked as I went to get a cup of coffee.

"Oh, he left with Neil early this morning. Neil woke Richard up and said the lawyer had changed the time of the appointment," she replied.

I went to sit beside her and said, "You will never guess what Neil did last night."

"I don't know Neil well enough to guess," Star said. "What did he do?"

"He kissed me on the lips," I said. "He wouldn't do that on a whim, would he?"

Star looked at me and said, "Trudy, the way I see Neil treating you, I don't think he'd hurt you. How do you feel about Neil? Was the kiss wrong?"

"Star, I love Neil, and it's not just because he rescued me. But that kiss did surprise me," I replied.

Just as I finished saying that, the boys came into the kitchen. They greeted us, then Ned asked where his father was.

"Good morning, Ned," I said. "Your father left with Uncle Neil. How did you sleep?"

"Good. Mom, I'm hungry. Would you make me some pancakes? Please?" Ned said. He went to sit at the table, and as he waited, he asked, "Where did they go?"

"They had to go meet a lawyer," Star replied.

Ned nodded.

Roger was not satisfied with the answer and asked, "Why would Uncle Neil and Dad go see a lawyer? Is something wrong?"

I looked at Star to see if she would answer, and when she didn't, I said, "They had to take care of something very special. Nothing is wrong. I'm sure they'll tell us all about it when they return."

I was relieved when they didn't ask any more questions.

Star went to work, and I drove the boys to school.

Wendy and I took care of the clinic, with Grant filling in for me in the afternoon, as usual. I don't think the time ever moved so slowly.

Just before we sat down to eat supper, Star got a call from Richard, who said he and Neil were on their way home.

When they arrived, a while after we'd finished eating, we were all at the door, waiting for them to come in.

Before they could even take their coats off, Star asked, "What did the lawyer say?"

"Let's all go sit down, and Neil will tell you," Richard said, giving Star a hello kiss.

We all went to sit in the living room.

Ned and I went to sit on the couch and much to my surprise, Neil came to sit beside me.

Everyone looked at Neil and waited for him to say something.

Anxious to know what he had found out, I asked, "Neil, aren't you going to tell us?"

Neil looked at me and said, "Yes, but I don't know where to start." He cleared his throat, then said, "This has been an overwhelming day. When we got to this lawyer's office, I thought that maybe it would be a hoax, Trudy, just like you said. His office was in the basement of a small apartment building, not very well maintained. When we entered the office, we were greeted by an elderly lady. I think she could have been his mother. She told us that Matt was on the phone and we should make ourselves comfortable. We waited for more than an hour. I was about to walk out when this jolly fellow came out of his office and introduced himself as Matt. After we told him who we were, he asked his secretary to get us some coffee and invited us into his office. You should have seen that office! I don't know how he knew where anything was. After we found a place to sit and had our coffee, Matt said, 'Well, let's get down to business. You must have a lot of questions. Let me say before we begin that I was following my client's wishes. I tried to advise her, but she never took my advice.'"

We were all sitting on the edge of our chairs as Neil kept telling us about the lawyer.

"Neil, what about the children? Tell us about them," I said impatiently.

"Yes, darling. I'm coming to that. I asked him where the children were, and he told us that the older children were with a good family friend and the newborn, a premature baby girl, was in the neonatal unit at the hospital."

When Star heard that, she gasped aloud, then asked, "How is the baby doing? Is she all right?"

"I'm not sure. The lawyer seemed to think she was doing okay," Richard replied.

"Do they know that you are their father?" I asked.

"Matt didn't know. He told us that he tried to advise Jill to tell the children about me, but she told him to do his lawyer thing and keep out of her affairs. They might not even know I exist. The couple taking care of the children now, want to adopt them," Neil said.

"Dad, what is Uncle Neil saying? Who are these children you're talking about?" Ned asked.

Richard looked at Roger and Ned and said, "I'm sorry. I should have told you guys about the kids before. These kids are your cousins. They are Uncle Neil's children."

"You mean we have cousins? Why didn't we know about them before?" Ned asked.

"Well, son, we just learned about them just yesterday. It's a little complicated," Richard replied, then he looked at the time and said, "It's getting late, and you two have school tomorrow. It's off to bed for you."

"Aw, Dad, I want to know more about these kids. Will they be coming to live here?" Ned asked.

"Ned, Uncle Neil will have to decide that. For now, it's time you were in bed. Come give me a good-night hug," Richard replied.

Ned very reluctantly went to give his father a hug. As he turned to go, I said, "I'll come tuck you in."

He took my hand, and we headed for his room.

As he was getting ready for bed, he never stopped talking. He was so excited about his newfound cousins, he could not settle down.

"Ned, say your prayers and get into bed," I said.

He knelt beside his bed and said, "Jesus, thank you for my cousins. Take care of them and keep them safe. Be with Mom and Dad and Roger and Star. Good night."

He usually kept going on, naming all the people he knew, but tonight he had his cousins on his mind.

Once he was in bed, I tucked him in and told him that I loved him. He closed his eyes and went to sleep.

When I returned, Richard and Neil were sitting at the dining room table, waiting for the snack Star was preparing.

When the food was set on the table, Neil said, "The lawyer told us that Jill liked to go to Las Vegas to gamble away her inheritance."

"Yes, he also told us that Amanda originally had that inheritance, and it went to Jill after Amanda died. Amanda never said a word to me about an inheritance. All she told me was that her parents were dead. I wonder what else she kept secret," Richard said.

"Richard, she must have had her reasons. Maybe the money held a bad memory, or maybe she loved that you could provide for her and that made her happy," Star said.

"Star, you're absolutely right. I'm not going to dwell on something I will never know," Richard said.

"So have you made plans as to when you'll go to get the kids?" I asked.

"The lawyer said that since I'm their father, I can go get them any time I want. But if they don't even know about me, it will be hard on them to be taken from the only place they've ever lived to come live with a perfect stranger. I'm thinking of going there to see them. Then, once they know me, I'll bring them here," Neil replied.

"I'm concerned about that newborn. We don't know how she is doing. I think the sooner you get there, the better," Star advised.

"Yes, I agree. We must decide who will be going, and when. What do you say, Richard?" Neil said.

"Well, that's your decision to make, Neil. I'll go with you, if you want," Richard said.

"Yes, thank you. I'd like that. Star, will you come too?" Neil asked.

"Yes, Neil, I want to see this newborn. I'll have to arrange time off with the school," Star replied.

"Okay, I think we have a plan. I'll call the lawyer and ask him to set up a visit with the kids for this weekend. Trudy, are you all right staying here and taking care of the boys and the clinic while we're away?" Neil asked.

"Yes, I'm okay with that. But I think Ned will be a little annoyed he's not going. He can't wait to meet his cousins," I said.

"I'll have a talk with him. I'll tell him he has to stay to help you prepare for the kids," Neil replied.

After Neil booked flights for them to fly out on the weekend, all was set. All that we needed to do now was tell the boys about the decision we had made.

I wasn't surprised to see Ned walking into the dining room early the next morning. He must have thought about his cousins all night long, for he was full of questions.

"Mom, do you know when Uncle Neil will be bringing the kids here? When they come, where are the kids going to sleep? Will they be staying with Uncle Neil, or will they stay here? Do you know their names? They must be younger than me, right, Mom?" Ned said.

After explaining that I didn't know the answers to most of his questions, I said, "Ned, you know as much as I do. Neil has not decided what to do yet. Now, please, no more questions. Dell has just put the pancakes in the heating tray. I'm going to have some; would you like some too?" I said.

We were eating when Richard and Star came in. A while later, Neil, Tex, Grant, and Wendy joined us. As we ate, Neil informed every one of the plan we had agreed to the night before. He asked Tex if Grant could put in more hours at the clinic while Neil was away.

"Do you know how long you will be gone?" Wendy asked.

"No, I don't know. It all depends on the children," Neil said.

I could see Ned was itching to ask a question, and when there was a lull in the conversation, he asked, "Dad, why can't I come?"

"Ned, your mother will need your help here. You might have to help set up for when they come. Speaking of which, Richard, would the children be able to stay here? That old house is not suited for them in its current state," Neil asked.

"The kids have a home here for as long as it takes. Ned, would you mind sharing your room?" Richard asked.

When Ned heard that he might have to share his room, he became very quiet. I could see he was turning it over in his mind.

"Dad, it would be all right. Just as long as they don't break my Legos," Ned finally replied.

That evening I heard a knock on my apartment door. When I answered it, I was surprised to see Neil. He had never been to my apartment before.

"Hey, Trudy. Can I come in?"

"Yes, Neil, of course. Is something wrong?" I asked, concerned that he was having trouble accepting that he now had four kids to care for.

He came in, and we went to sit on the couch.

"No, Trudy, nothing is wrong. I just want to talk. I've been thinking this over for a long time," he said.

Now, my curiosity piqued, I asked, "What is it Neil? Does this concern the children?"

"No, it concerns you and me. Oh, Trudy, I don't know how to put this," Neil said, moving closer to me. He took my hand and said, "Would you date a guy with four kids?"

The question took me off guard. "You want to date me? Why would you ask me this now?"

That must not have been what he wanted to hear, for he started to stand.

I held on to his hand and said, "Neil, if I liked the guy, I'd date him even if he had ten kids."

"Trudy, you would? I was going to ask you out as soon as I was divorced. Now I don't need a divorce, but I have four kids, I don't think there'll ever be a good time to ask you. I don't want to wait any longer. So, Trudy, where would you like to go for our first date?" Neil said.

Before I could answer, he brought me close, and we kissed. Staying in our embrace, I replied, "Neil, what if we took the horses and went for a ride down to the meadow where you had your horses? I'd like that. We have not gone for a ride in a long time."

Neil looked at me, gave me a quick kiss and said, "I was thinking of bringing you to a fancy restaurant in town. But I like your idea better. It will be great to go riding again. We'll ask Star to bring the boys to school, so we can head out early then you'll be back in time to go get the boys.

"Oh, I'm glad you agree. I'll pack a lunch, and we'll eat it when we get there," I said.

We kissed again then he said, "Good night, darling. See you tomorrow."

After he left, I thought about his visit. I could not remember ever feeling that happy. Neil wanted me; he had not said that he loved me, but I was sure that he would in time.

The weather was perfect for our date ride. Neil rode Rae, and I rode Bell. After working with her all winter, I felt confident sitting on her. We followed the natural path the animals used to go to the meadow. As we rode, Neil told me about how his father had bought the ranch and how, as a little boy, he had explored just about every inch of it. When we got to the meadow, I put out a blanket on the grass and set our picnic on it. As we sat close together admiring the scenery, we ate our lunch.

After we finished eating, Neil said, "We're not far from the place where I found you."

"No, that can't be. The creek is not even close to here," I declared.

"I know. I could show you the tree I found you in," Neil replied.

A cold shiver ran down my back, and I said, "Neil, I don't want to see that. Please let's go back home."

Neil gathered me in his arms and said, "I'm so sorry, Trudy. I should have kept my big mouth shut. I never realized you didn't know where I found you."

He sounded so apologetic, I felt bad for asking to go back.

I loved having Neil's arms around me, so I said, "Neil, I'm sorry. I think I overreacted. Maybe you could show me another time. Let's just enjoy this moment."

When it was time for us to return home, I walked to Bell and was going to get on her, but Rae came beside her and pushed her away.

"Rae, what are you doing? Leave Bell alone," Neil scolded his horse.

But Rae would not let me get near Bell. He stood in front of me and kept nodding his head.

"Trudy, I think he wants you to ride him," Neil said.

I looked at him and said, "No way. After what he did to Richard, I'm not getting on your horse."

Neil went to his horse and whispered something in his ear. Rae pawed the ground with his hoof and nodded his head.

"It's not the same," Neil said. "Richard never asked if he could ride him. Rae wants you to ride him. He'll let you. Get on; he'll be good. I know him, and he's never let me down."

"Are you 100 percent sure, Neil?" I asked.

When Neil said that he was, I took the reins, and with Neil's help I got on the horse. Rae stood very still as Neil adjusted the stirrups. Then, Neil got on Bell, and we started for home.

As we rode, Rae started into a fast trot. At first, I was a little scared, but I soon realized he wanted to show me what he could do. He was such a marvelous horse, giving me the smoothest ride I had ever experienced. I relaxed and enjoyed it.

When we got to the barn, Neil helped me off his horse and said, "I could tell you enjoyed the ride. He was showing off for you, you know."

Before I could say anything, Rae neighed and pushed Neil into me.

Neil held on to me, and we kissed.

Then, Neil turned to the horse and said, "Yes, Rae, I've asked her. Now please leave me to court Trudy the way I want to. I don't need your help."

"Neil, it sounds so funny when you talk to him like that. Does he understand what you're saying?" I asked.

Neil smiled and said, "Rae thinks I'm like him. He likes you, and he wants me to like you too. He's always putting his nose in my affairs."

We were walking back to the house when I asked, "When are we going to tell the family that we're dating? Ned might not be happy; he had trouble accepting Star dating Richard."

"Trudy, no worries. I've already passed it by him," Neil said.

For a minute, I could not believe what he had just said. "When did you talk to Ned?"

Neil laughed and said, "That little boy loves you so much, he'd do anything for you. I had a talk with him the day before I received the letter."

"But that was three days ago! He never said a word to me. Did you swear him to secrecy?"

"I told him to keep it to himself. I think he wanted me to surprise you."

"Yes, that sounds like Ned. He would never want to spoil a surprise."

Friday morning came, and Richard, Star, and Neil left very early to catch their flight. The boys and I were up to wish them goodbye.

After the three left, I felt a sense of apprehension. There were so many things we did not know. The home life the boys had was about to change, and I prayed it would not be for the worse. Neil had an introductory letter from the lawyer to show the couple caring for the children. I hoped that they would accept it and not cause him any trouble.

Our day went by like any other, but we all wished Neil would call to tell us how things were going.

Ned was not happy having to go to bed not knowing. When I tucked him in, he said, "Mom, did Uncle Neil answer your text?" I told him that he hadn't, so he said, "When Uncle Neil calls, will you wake me up? I want to know what he says."

"Okay, dear, I will. Now go to sleep," I said.

I went to watch TV and waited for Neil to answer me. After waiting until it was past midnight, I went to bed. As I lay in bed, unable to sleep, I prayed that everything was all right with all of them.

In the morning, when Ned got up, he looked upset, so I asked, "What's the matter, Ned?"

"You never woke me, Mom. Why?" he replied.

When I told him that Neil had not gotten in touch with me, Ned said he was sorry for being grumpy, then asked for something to eat.

Another day passed without any word from Neil or Richard. Then, on Sunday morning, Neil called to tell us that he was bringing the twins and the little girl home that night. We tried to get Neil to say more, but he told us he had the kids with him and could not talk any longer.

"Well, boys, that means we have to get this place ready for them. Where do you think we should sleep them?" I said. I looked at the two boys, expecting an answer, but they said nothing. All they did was stare at me. "Don't you have any suggestions?"

"Mom, I could move my things to the downstairs room. I always wanted to have that room, but Dad said I had to be older before I could be downstairs by myself. I don't think Dad would mind, now that I'm older," Roger replied.

"Yes, Roger, that is the solution. I'll get Grant and Tex to come help us," I said.

"I could take Roger's room and move my things into it. The twins could have my room, with the bunk beds, and we could set up a little bed for the girl. Would that be okay?" Ned suggested.

When Grant and Tex came, they helped the boys move their things and set up a bed for the little girl. Ned was very pleased that we had accepted his suggestions.

As Ned helped me make the beds, he said, "When do you think they'll get here? Do you think they'll like living here?"

"Ned, it will be pretty late when they get here. As for them liking to live here, time will tell. But I hope they do," I said.

I was able to convince Ned to go to bed by promising him that I'd wake him up the minute Neil arrived with the kids. I was reading when Neil called to say that they would be home within the hour.

A half hour before Neil was to arrive, I went to wake Ned and told him that Neil would be home soon. We were both waiting at the door when the car came to a stop. I saw Neil lift the little girl out of the car and carry her to the door. The boys followed in his wake.

When he got close to me, Neil gave me a quick kiss on the cheek and said, "Do you have a bed ready for this little princess?"

I told him to follow me and showed him to the bed we had prepared for the little girl. The twin boys were right behind him. Neil placed the little girl in bed without waking her up.

"Come, boys, let's go to the living room. We don't want to wake your sister," Neil whispered as he led them out of the room.

Once we were in the living room, Neil introduced us to the twins, but he did not say which boy was which. When I looked at them, I thought I was seeing double.

I smiled at them, but before I could say anything, Ned said, "They have my dad's name and your name, Uncle Neil?"

The boys looked at Ned, and one of them said, "You have the same green eyes as we do. I'm Richard."

Without missing a beat, the other boy jumped in and said, "I'm Neil."

"Well, it's very nice to meet you both. You must be hungry. Why don't we go to the kitchen and find something to eat?" I said.

They all followed me to the kitchen, and when the three boys were seated at the counter, I asked, "How about toast and some milk? Would that be okay?"

The twins nodded.

Ned sat there, looking at his cousins, I could see he was itching to ask them questions but kept quiet. They had just finished eating when Tex came in, carrying their luggage. I saw the boys' eyes grow big as they watched Tex come up to them.

"Are you a real cowboy?" Richard asked.

"Yeah, I suppose you could say I am. It sure is good to see you two. You look just like your dad did when he was a boy. I'm Tex. Now what do I call you?" Tex said, looking at the boys.

After Neil made the introductions, Tex gave Neil a surprised look, then said, "Well, I'll be! I'm pleased to meet you two. It's past my bedtime, so I'll say good night."

I saw Tex shake his head as he walked away.

Neil bid Tex good night, then turned to the boys and said, "Well, boys, it's very late. We'd better get you two to bed."

The boys went to get their bags, and we all headed upstairs. Ned showed them their room and where the bathroom was. Once the twins had their pajamas on and their teeth brushed, they got in their beds, the instant their heads touched their pillows, they were asleep.

Once the twins were in bed, Ned went to his room. I followed him so I could tuck him in. As he laid in bed, he looked at me and said, "It's so strange, their names. Why would their mother give them those names?"

I sat on the side of his bed and said, "Ned it's very late and you have a big day ahead of you tomorrow. You can find out all you want to know in the morning. Now it's time you went to sleep. Good night my boy." As I stood up, I gave him a quick kiss on the forehead and went downstairs.

When I returned to the kitchen, I saw that Neil had made some nighttime tea.

As we sat at the counter, sipping our tea, I said, "The boys have your looks. How is that possible?"

He played with the tea bag in his cup and said, "Jill must have been pregnant when she left and never told me she was. I just don't know how she could have lied to those boys for this long. I don't know how little Amanda came along, though."

"The little girl's name is Amanda? It's like Jill was trying to re-create her family," I said.

"Yes, it's pretty weird. I think there must have been something wrong with her," Neil's voice sounded so filled with pain, almost like he had been beaten up.

"I'm sorry. It must be hard to know that someone you once loved could hurt you so badly," I said.

"She was trying to hurt me, but I think she hurt the boys even more. Those kids are so loving and trusting. I don't know why Jill would not tell me about them," Neil replied.

"Tell me about the couple who was taking care of them," I said.

"They were a very nice older couple, Dave and Susan. The kids called them Grandma and Grandpa. I'm glad that they were there to take care of them. The boys told me that they liked going there because when they were there, they got more to eat," Neil replied.

"Did you get to see the little baby girl? How is she doing?" I asked.

"Well I didn't get a good look at her. She was in an incubator and had all kinds of tubes going into her. The nurse taking care of her said that she's holding her own," Neil replied as he yawned then said, "Trudy, I'm bushed. This has been a very trying day. I must get some shut eye. We'll have more time to talk tomorrow. I'll sleep in the guest room tonight. Is that okay?"

"Yes, I thought you would want to. It's ready for you," I replied. "I can sleep in the apartment if you're here to keep an eye on the kids."

He stood up, and after we kissed, he said good night.

14

The next morning, I was having coffee with Dell when Neil walked into the kitchen.

As he went to get himself some coffee, he greeted me with a pleasant, "Good morning, darling, you're up early." He came to sit by me, and as he did, he gave me a quick kiss on the lips.

Dell saw us kiss and smiled at us.

"Is there something you're not telling me?" she asked as she took a sip of her coffee.

With the biggest grin on his face, Neil said, "Trudy and I are dating."

"Well, it's about time. Tex and I had a wager on how long it would take before you two got together," Dell replied.

I was about to ask who won the wager, when we heard a loud scream.

"What in the world is that?" Neil said as he rushed out of the room and ran toward the stairs.

I was right behind him. When we got to the room, little Amanda was sitting in bed, crying her little heart out.

"Hey, little Amanda. I'm here; you don't have to worry," Neil said as he sat on the bed.

Amanda came to sit on his lap and cuddled up to him.

Neil wiped away her tears and said, "You got scared? Waking up in a strange place does that to me too."

She nodded and cuddled closer to him, then looked at me, and in her sweet little voice said, "Who is that lady?"

"Amanda, this is the nice lady I told you about. Her name is Trudy. She loves children and takes very good care of them. She's our nanny," Neil replied.

"A nanny? Like Mary Poppins?" she asked.

Both Neil and I laughed.

"Yes, something like that, but I don't fly or do magic," I replied.

Amanda smiled, then said she had to go to the bathroom.

"Would you like me to take you there?" I asked.

She nodded and came to take my hand. When we returned, we found all the boys in Ned's room. Neil was sitting on the bed, watching Ned and the twins examine the big Lego building Ned had built. I could tell that Ned just loved having them ask about how he had built it.

I watched them for a while, then said, "Ned, today is Track and Field Day at school. We should go have breakfast if you want to get there on time."

"Can Richard and Neil come?" Ned asked.

I looked at the boys and said, "Yes everyone can come, it's a family day. All brothers, sisters, moms, and dads are all welcomed."

"Well, boys, you heard the lady. Go get dressed. We'll meet you all downstairs for breakfast," Neil said.

We were having breakfast when Roger walked into the room. When the kids saw him, they stopped eating.

Amanda said, "There's another big boy here? What's your name?"

Roger smiled and said, "I'm Roger, and who are you, pretty girl?"

She looked at him, as if she were captivated by his words.

"That's Amanda. I'm Neil, and that's my brother, Richard," little Neil replied, then asked, "Are you coming to Track and Field Day with us?"

I saw a puzzled look come over Roger's face as he said, "That's my mother's name?" looking at Neil for an answer.

"Do you remember your mother had a sister, Jill? She was my wife," Neil replied.

"Oh, I don't remember Jill. I was very little when my mother went away," Roger replied. He went to get himself some breakfast and as he did, he shook his head and said, "That's so weird." When he returned to the table, he went to sit beside Amanda.

While Roger ate, little Neil asked again, "Are you coming to Track and Field Day with us?"

"Yes, I am. It should be a lot of fun," Roger replied. As he ate, he asked, "When are Dad and Star coming back?"

"I don't know. It depends on the baby. Star said she wanted to stay there until the baby is big enough to come home," Neil replied.

"How long will that take?" Roger asked. "Will Star be the one who takes care of the baby when she gets home?"

"I don't know. We haven't determined that yet; we'll have to see," Neil said.

With Neil's help, I packed all the things we would need for the school outing. When we had everything ready, we all piled into the Suburban and set out. On the way there, the twins kept asking all kinds of questions, and Ned was only too happy to answer them.

Once at school, Ned brought the twins with him to his class. I went with them, in case there were questions he would not be able to answer.

When all the kids were seated, the teacher greeted them and said, "We have new boys with us today. Ned, would you like to introduce them?"

"Yes, ma'am. These are my cousins, Richard and Neil. They just moved here," Ned answered.

"Welcome, boys. Class, say hello to Richard and Neil," the teacher said.

All the children in the class shouted a big hello.

"Okay, class, today is our Track and Field Day. It's a fun day, and I want everyone to enjoy themselves. Let's go outside and join the others. Have fun!"

Before the teacher could say more, the kids stood up and ran out the door.

Volunteers had planned the day, organizing all kinds of games that involved both adults and children. Ned and I competed in a three-legged race. We came in second; Trevor and Liz beat us by just a few inches. We all cheered when Roger won in the high jump. The Lance family competed in the beanbag toss. Amanda just loved it when Neil asked her to throw the beanbag for him. We did not win the competition, but we certainly had a lot of fun. The boys were in most of the competitions and brought home all kinds of ribbons. We were enjoying ourselves, but we were very pleased when we saw they were serving the potluck picnic.

I set out a large blanket on the grass, so all our crew would be able to sit together to have lunch. Everyone had to bring a plate, so I handed the boys their plates, and they headed to the food table. Once we had our food, we ate in silence, too exhausted to say much.

After lunch, there were more races, but I decided to opt out. Amanda had fallen asleep in Neil's arms, so I went to sit beside him and watch the boys compete.

"Look at you! You look like an old hand doing this," I commented.

Neil smiled and in a soft voice said, "This feels so nice. These kids are such a blessing. I'm really enjoying this." He looked down at Amanda and brushed a stray hair from her face.

"It's nice to see that Ned and Roger have accepted the twins so easily," Neil said.

"Did you think that they wouldn't get along? Ned can't stop talking about his cousins. He's very happy to have them here. I think the twins will be good for him," I replied, then asked, "How was their reaction when they first saw you? Did they know about you?"

"When we first got to Dave and Susan's place, the kids were out playing with the neighbors' kids, so we were able to talk to them without the children being there. Susan told us that the children knew their mother had died and that she would not be coming back. She said that when the lawyer called to say that the father wanted the children, she was very surprised. You see, Jill had never told her about me. Then, she went on to tell us that Jill would leave the kids with them and go to Las Vegas for weeks at a time. The last time Jill went there, she was badly beaten up and never went there again. Susan said she did not even know that Jill was pregnant this last time until the day she went into labor. One can only wonder what could have happened to her," Neil explained.

"So what happened when you met the kids? They must have been very surprised," I said.

"At first, the boys were a little unsure of me. They asked why I had not come for them before. I had to tell them that Jill had never told me about them. Then, I explained what happened the night she left and told them that I had tried to find her but was never able to. Little Neil, who's quite clever, looked at me and said, 'Mom was away a lot and left us with Grandma and Grandpa. She told us she had to go to work. We were hungry all the time when we were at home. When we asked her where our father was, she told us we were better off without him.' Then, without even blinking, he asked, 'Will we be coming to live with you now?'" Neil said.

Little Amanda woke up and ended our conversation.

"Hey, Amanda, do you want to go play with the other kids now?" Neil asked.

She shook her head and said, "I don't feel good. My tummy hurts, and my head hurts."

She rubbed her tummy, and for a second, I thought that she was going to be sick.

Neil felt her forehead and said, "She's burning up; let's get her inside. She might be suffering from heatstroke."

Once we were inside the school, I went to get her a cup of cold water.

After Amanda had a drink, she said she felt better, but Neil thought it would be best if we went home.

I agreed, so I went to find the boys, leaving Neil to care for Amanda.

When we got home, everyone was exhausted, but we all agreed it had been a very fun day. The boys had many ribbons, but Roger was the only one to have a first-place ribbon.

Little Amanda made sure everyone knew that she had won two ribbons also.

I heated up the chicken casserole Dell had made for us. Then went to make a salad. Ned was helping me with the salad when I looked at his hair. "You have sand in your hair; you need a bath. Why don't you go now while supper is cooking?" I said.

"Okay, Mom," he said and ran out of the kitchen.

When Ned finished his bath, he returned to the kitchen, and we all sat down for supper.

After supper, Neil said to the twins, "I think you two should take a bath. Who wants to go first?"

"You mean, we don't have to take a bath together? Mom always made us take baths together. Neil likes to lie down in the tub, and I never have any room," Richard said.

"Yes, that's right you can each have your own bath. Do you want to go first?" Neil asked.

When Richard said yes, Neil went and showed him how to run the bath.

Little Neil waited, I could tell that he was not amused; he clearly did not like having to wait for his brother.

When Richard had finished his bath and got out of the bathroom, little Neil said, "It's about time. I thought you had drowned in there."

Once little Neil had his bath, I asked Amanda if she wanted one.

She nodded, so I took her and helped her bathe.

As she played in the water, I asked, "How are you feeling now, Amanda?"

"I feel good, my tummy feels better," she said, then looked at me and said, "My mom is gone. Ned said I could call you Mom. Are you my mommy now?"

I was not expecting the question. It took me a few seconds to know how to answer her. I gave her a big smile and said, "Well, Amanda, I'm your nanny. Why don't we see what your daddy says?"

She nodded and continued to play with the water toys.

With the kids in bed, Neil and I went outside to enjoy the beautiful evening.

We were sitting on the porch swing when Neil said, "Boy! What a day! No one would believe what I did today; imagine me, with three kids at a school event. Single guys just don't do things like that."

"But you had a good time, didn't you?" I asked.

"Yes, it brought back a lot of childhood memories. It's nice to know that some things don't change. How about you, darling, did you enjoy yourself?" he asked as he drew me closer to him.

"I did. It's so lovely to see kids enjoying themselves. There should be more days like this one. I wonder what the kids really thought about today. It must feel strange to them to suddenly have a new family."

"Yes, it must, but kids are adaptable. They'll be all right," Neil replied.

"I hope so. When I was giving Amanda her bath, she told me that Ned had told her to call me Mom. How do you feel about that?" I asked, uncertain of what he was going to say.

He smiled and said, "It's okay by me. You're the only mother they'll ever have from now on."

The answer surprised me. He seemed so sure of himself, so I asked, "Did you know that Ned told the kids to call me Mom?

"Yes, it was Richard who asked. He did not think calling you by your name was right. You were Mom to Ned, so he thought, since he lived in the same house, you should be Mom to him too. I'm okay with it."

"Well, okay, if you say it is," I said, surprised by his decision.

I felt overwhelmed by the idea of being a mother to four kids. Then, I thought, *What about the newborn? Will I have to care for her too?*

We swung for a while, then I asked, "Have you heard from Richard?"

"No. I guess there must be no change in the baby. I'm sure he would call if there had been."

"Yes, I suppose. Did you have any trouble to get to see the baby?" I asked.

He put his arm around my shoulders and said, "Yes, we did. At first, the hospital would not let us see her until I showed them the letter from the lawyer. Once they saw the letter, they would only allow two of us in at a time, so Star and I went. I have never seen a baby so small; she couldn't have been bigger than my hand. All I could see was that she had a lot of dark hair. Poor little thing was in an incubator, connected to a lot of tubes. We were standing there, looking at this little thing, when I heard Star say, 'Hi, little one! Oh, please keep on fighting. You're not alone anymore; I'm here for you now.' Then, Star looked at me and asked me if I would let her take care of the baby."

"Is that when you decided to come home with the kids and have Richard and Star stay?"

"Well, that was all Star's doing. When I told the kids that I wanted them to come live with me on the ranch, they did not want to wait. So Star suggested that I take the kids and that she and Richard would stay to care for the baby. After she saw the baby, she did not want to leave her. That night, at the motel, she asked me if she could adopt her. It came so out of left field, I didn't know what to say. Then, she said, 'I guess it's too early to make a decision like that. We'll talk again later.' And do you know when later was? The next morning! We were having breakfast when she asked, 'Neil, did you make your decision yet? I know that this little girl is meant to be ours. Please let us adopt her.' She was so emotional, she had tears rolling down her cheeks, but Richard told me to take my time deciding. I've been thinking about it, and I have this strong feeling she should be Star's. But I haven't said anything to them yet," Neil replied.

"When are you going to tell them?"

"I think I'll tell them when they bring the baby home."

"Do the boys know about the baby?"

"Yes, they know. Susan told them."

"For Star's sake, I pray that the baby survives. She's wanted children for a long time, I know she'll be a great mother," I said.

Neil agreed but did not say more.

I was tired, so I put my head on Neil's shoulder and closed my eyes. I don't know how long I slept, but when I woke up, Neil said, "Darling, you have got to go to bed. You must be very tired after all you did today. Let me walk you to your apartment."

He helped me to my feet, and I took his arm.

When we got to the door, Neil brought me close, and we kissed.

As we ended the kiss, I said, "I love you. You know, sometimes I wish—"

Before I could finish what I had started to say, Neil kissed me again. Then, he said good night and returned to the house.

School closed for the summer, and with Richard and Star gone, my nanny duties were full time, all day and all night. Tex and Roger took the horses on the rodeo circuit. With them away, it seemed like the rest of us had twice as many duties. Grant oversaw the ranch operations and couldn't always come to relieve me at the clinic. Neil would do most of his work in the morning, so I took care of the kids then, and would go to the clinic in the afternoon. Three days after the kids arrived, Neil and Grant were both away when it came time for me to go to work, so I took the kids to the clinic. The boys were very restless and would not listen to me, so I told them to go play in the arena. A while later they were back, and they all had tears in their eyes.

When I saw them, I became alarmed and asked, "What happened? Why are you crying? Are you hurt?"

"Mom, I spooked Bella, and she reared up and just about hit Neil in the head with her hoof," Richard cried.

I went to see if little Neil had any injuries and when I asked him if he was okay, he nodded. I looked at Ned and asked, "You had Bella? Why did you have the horse? What happened, Ned?

"Mom, it's not Ned's fault; it's mine. I wanted to lead Bella, but Neil would not let me. It was my turn to lead her, so I yelled at him. That's when Bella got scared and reared up," Richard said through his tears.

"Oh, I see. But why did you have the horse?" I asked.

"We were bored, and I thought if we got the horses, we'd have something to do. I'm sorry, Mom; I just didn't think anything would happen. I've done this so many times before," Ned said, then added, "Bell and Bella are in the paddocks in the arena."

"Boys, we're all overworked. I'll see when Neil will be home. Until he gets here, please go sit in those chairs."

With their heads down, they all turned and went to sit.

I went to find Wendy and told her I was going home. She said that was okay, as Grant would be returning home soon; she would call him if she needed help.

When I returned to the boys, they were all quiet and looked like a sorry lot.

"Let's go to the house," I said. "Neil said he'll be home soon."

I took little Amanda's hand, and as I stepped out the door, Richard took my other hand. As we walked to the main house, I could feel that Richard was still shaking. Ned and little Neil walked along behind us.

When Neil came home a short time later, the boys were sitting quietly at the dining room table.

As soon as he saw them, Neil said, "Why all the sad faces? Who die?"

"I did something really bad, Dad," Richard said, trying hard to stop his tears.

"What happened? I see that everyone is okay, so it can't be that bad," Neil replied.

Little Neil sat up straight and recounted the story to his dad. When Neil heard the story, I saw his face change expression.

He went to sit at the table with the boys and said, "Well, that was a close call, and we never want to have another one. We will have to set some rules. Horses are skittish animals; just about anything can set them off. I'm glad that you are okay, Neil. Let's go help Mom with supper. We'll talk about this later."

After supper, Neil took the boys and went over the rules he wanted them to follow. The boys all agreed that they would follow them.

After the kids were in bed, Neil came to sit beside me as I went over the clinic books.

"Put those away, Trudy. You've done enough for today. We can't keep going like this. I must hire a receptionist. I'm going to call the animal hospital in the city and see if they know of someone who can help us out on a short-term basis. I talked to Richard last night. He said that the baby is doing better with them there, but it might take all month before they can bring her home. We need help. From now on, your only job is to take care of the kids. No more clinic for now," Neil said.

I felt such a relief, I turned, hugged Neil, and said, "Thank you, so much! Lately, I've been juggling so many things and not handling any of them very well. I should never have left the boys alone."

"No, Trudy, you were doing the best you could. The kids should have been your priority, but I made it impossible for you to do that," Neil replied.

The following afternoon the boys asked if they could go see the horses. When I said they could, they rushed off to the barn. Amanda and I followed. Ned and little Neil went to brush the horses, but Richard went to sit on a bale to watch them.

Amanda and I went to sit beside him, and I asked, "Don't you want to go brush the horse?"

He shook his head, so I asked, "Richard, what's the matter? Why do you look so sad?"

He looked at me and then fell into my arms, crying. "Mom, I do stupid things sometimes; I don't know why. Neil could have been hurt yesterday. Do you think Dad will let me stay here?"

"Oh! Richard, your dad loves you very much. He'll never want you to leave. Do you want to go talk to him? He's at the clinic now; let's go see if he's busy," I said.

"Okay, Mom. Do you think he would mind?" he asked.

"No, Richard, he won't mind; he'll make time for you. We'll saddle the horses, so Ned and Neil can ride, then we'll go see your dad," I said.

After I saddled the horses, we all headed for the clinic. When we got there, Ned and little Neil went to ride in the arena, while Richard, Amanda, and I went to find Neil.

When I told Neil that Ned and little Neil were riding in the arena, he said, "Let's go see how they're doing. Richard, we can talk while we're watching them. Is that okay with you?"

"Yes, Dad, it's okay," Richard replied.

When we got to the arena, we went to sit on a bale and watched as the boys put the horses through their paces.

"Dad, do you want me here?" Richard asked.

Neil's facial expression immediately showed concern, and he said, "Of course I want you here. Why would you ask me that?"

"Because of what I did," Richard replied.

Neil brought him close and gave him a hug. "You are my son. A few days ago, I did not know about you. Now that you're here, I will never want you to go anywhere."

They sat close together for a while, then Richard said, "Dad, I'm scared of horses now. When Bella reared up, she looked so big. I scared her. She probably hates me now."

"Well, the only way to find out is to go see. Horses are forgiving. You could bring her a treat; she would like that. Do you want to do that?" Neil said.

Richard looked at Neil and said, "No, not today. I'll sleep on it."

Sunday came, and I could not believe that the kids had been with us for only a week. It felt more like a month. I was thankful that God had given me the strength to go through it.

As we ate breakfast, I told the twins that we were going to

church. They stared at me as if I had told them we were going to the moon.

Then, in a meek voice little Neil asked, "What is church?"

"You don't know what church is?" Ned asked.

Both twins said no, so Ned explained what church was.

Although Neil had only attended church at Christmas, he told his children that we would all be going. Once there, the twins followed Ned to the kids' service, while Neil, Amanda, and I went to the regular service.

Amanda did not want to go with the boys and asked to stay with Neil. She sat on Neil's lap through the entire service. She was definitely getting to be Daddy's girl.

In the week that followed, we establish a routine. Neil hired two students from the veterinary school, making the workload at the clinic much easier.

After being away for a couple of weeks, Richard called to say he was coming home.

When he arrived home and Ned saw him, he ran to him and jumped into his arms.

"Dad, I've missed you so much. Where is Star?" Ned asked.

"Star is staying with the baby until she is big enough to come home. How are you doing, son?" Richard asked as he put Ned down.

"Oh, really good, Dad, but I missed you; you were away for a long time. Neil, Richard, say hi to my dad," Ned said.

The twins greeted him, then Richard said, "Hello, boys. How do you like living here?"

"We like it here, Uncle Richard. It's so much better than living in a city," little Neil replied.

After a few more questions, Richard turned his attention to Neil, so the boys and I left them to carry on their business.

That evening, while we ate supper, Richard informed us that he would be going to join Tex and Roger on the rodeo circuit.

When Ned heard this, he asked, "Dad, can I come?"

"Yes, I suppose you can. I haven't spent much time with you lately," Richard replied.

I could tell that Ned was overjoyed for I knew it would make him happy to be with his father. It pleased me to know that they would be spending time together.

The day Richard and Ned left was very sad for me and the twins. With Ned gone, the twins looked lost; they did not seem to know what to do with themselves.

"Well, boys, what would you like to do?" I asked.

They both looked at me and shrugged their shoulders.

Then, Neil said, "I wish I could have gone with Ned."

A second later, Richard said, "Me too."

"Oh, you do, do you? Well, we can still have fun here," I said with enthusiasm. "Why don't we go see the horses?"

"No. I don't want to. I'll just go to my room," Neil said and went into the house.

Richard looked at me and asked, "Mom, can I go watch some cartoons?"

"Okay, Richard, if that's what you want," I replied.

I was at a loss to know what to do. I went to see if Amanda had woken from her nap, but she hadn't, so I went to find Richard and watched cartoons with him.

Later, when Neil came home from work, he asked the twins to help him care for the horses. They suddenly revived and were happy to go with him. I guessed they did not think much of my company.

As the week went by, the twins continued being cold toward me.

After Neil went to work on Friday, I found little Neil in Ned's room. He had taken one of Ned's prize Lego vans apart. When he saw me, he quickly tried to hide what he had done.

"Neil, what have you done? Ned would be very upset with you. Why would you do this?" I asked.

He looked at me and cried, "I don't care about Ned. He gets everything." He then ran out of the room.

I stood there, utterly surprised, and thought, *Oh my! I think we have a problem. The twins are not as happy as we thought they were.*

When I called the kids to come to the table for lunch, only Richard and Amanda came.

"Where's Neil?" I asked Richard.

"I don't know, Mom," Richard replied. "I was playing with Amanda. Neil wasn't with us."

My heart sank. *Where could he have gone?*

I called Grant, told him that little Neil was missing, and asked if he had seen him. When he told me he hadn't, I became very concerned.

I should have gone after him when he ran out of Ned's room, I thought. *Neil will have my head if something has happened to little Neil. Not to mention that I'd never forgive myself.*

I was about to call Neil when Grant and little Neil walked into the house. I was so happy to see little Neil. I went to give him a hug, but he pushed me away and ran to his room.

After I thanked Grant for bringing little Neil back, I asked, "Where was he?"

Grant smiled and said, "He was trying to saddle Bell, and when he saw me, he asked me to help. If you hadn't called me, I would've helped him. What's with him, anyway? He said he wanted to get away from here."

"I think he has his nose a little out of joint because Richard took Ned with him," I replied.

"Yeah, that sounds like what little boys would do. He'll get over it. It's just sibling rivalry," Grant said with a grin on his face.

Little Neil stayed in his room until his father called him for supper.

As we ate, Neil saw that little Neil was not happy, so he asked, "Neil, why the sad face? Did you lose your fortune?"

Little Neil looked at me. I guess he wanted me to tell Neil what he had done, but all I did was smile at him. *I'm not going to tell; you're on your own, boy,* I thought.

"Neil, what happened? Why is everyone so quiet?" Neil asked as he looked at me.

I kept on eating and did not say anything.

"Neil, I know there's something going on here. Why are you not telling me?"

Richard looked at me and was about to say something, but I stopped him with a shake of my head.

We had finished eating when little Neil asked, "Dad, why couldn't I go with Ned? Why was he able to go, but I wasn't?"

"You wanted to go with Ned? Ned went with Uncle Richard because Ned is Richard's son and he wanted to be with him. You are my son, and I want you with me," Neil replied.

"Then, why is Ned always with us? Is Star his mom?" little Neil asked.

I looked at little Neil and said, "Ned is my son. Star is his stepmother. I know it's hard to figure out, Neil, but Ned belongs to both families."

"Neil, you are as important as anyone else in this family. Trudy and I love you, and we want you to be happy. Are you mad at Ned because he went with his dad?" Neil asked.

"Yes, Dad," he cried. Then, with big tears in his eyes he said, "Trudy caught me breaking Ned's Lego, so I wanted to run away. I didn't think you'd want me anymore."

"Neil, Richard, you two are my sons. You'll always be my sons. I missed six years out of your lives, and I don't want to miss any more. Now, Neil, I think there's someone you have to apologize to."

"Apologize? What's that?" little Neil asked.

"It's when you say you're sorry," Richard said. "Mom was very worried about you. You should be nicer to her and stop being jealous of Ned."

It was the first time I saw a real division between the boys. It made me fully aware that although they looked alike, they were very different.

At bedtime, as I was tucking in little Neil, he said, "I'm sorry for what I did today. I was so mad at you because you did not ask Uncle Richard to take me. I was thinking of never calling you Mom, but I changed my mind. You're a good mother; not like the mother we had before. I'm sorry, Mom."

I took him in my arms and said, "Neil, I forgive you. Why didn't you ask Uncle Richard if you could go with them?"

"Mom, I was too scared to ask him. I don't know Ned's dad; I had only met him once before he came back here," he replied.

"Well, you're here with your dad and me. We love having you here," I said.

He smiled at me, said good night, and went to sleep.

Once the boys were in bed, I went to find Neil. He was sitting on one of the La-Z-Boys, so I went to sit beside him.

"Well, I'm sure happy this week is over and that we got to the bottom of what was troubling the boys. I didn't like the way they were treating me."

"How were they treating you?" Neil asked. "I never noticed anything odd."

That did not surprise me, for the twins were always polite to me when Neil was around.

"Well, Neil, they were a little cold towards me, I felt that they never wanted to spend much time with me. As for Little Neil, I don't think he'll do that again. He said he was sorry and told me he like me as his mother. I'm pretty sure Little Richard feels the same. I'm very tired. I'm going to bed. Good night, Neil."

I moved closer and kissed him. As I did, he pulled me onto his lap and said, "Trudy, have I told you that I love you?"

I looked at him and said, "Oh, you have now. I love you too."

He brought me close and we kissed.

A week later, on Sunday evening, Neil and I were swinging on the porch swing when he said, "The pastor's sermon was very interesting this morning. I liked what he said about how Jesus still works miracles today. I've been thinking about that all day. If you look back at this family, you can see the miracles He's done. The first big one was Richard's conversion. Richard would never go to church as a boy. He was always his own man, even as a youngster; he never thought he needed anyone to help him. Then, there's you coming here to be Ned's mother. Ned told me he prayed for a mom for a long time. The miracle that affected me the most is how I found you in that creek. I was ready to give up the search, but I suddenly felt I should go just a little farther. When I saw you on that tree, I did not think anyone could have lived through that."

"I'm so glad you listened to that sensation," I said. He nodded, and asked, "Did you see the picture Star sent of the baby?"

"Yes. She's so cute and so tiny."

"That's another big miracle. Did you notice the baby has a widow's peak, the same kind of hairline Star has? And did you notice the shape of her eyes and mouth? They're very similar to Star's. I think that the baby was meant to be Richard and Star'," Neil said.

"Yes, I did notice, but I thought I was just imagining what I saw," I replied.

"Jill tried to hurt me by keeping the children away from me, but God turned that hate into a blessing. I thank Him every day for bringing those kids into my life. You would have to be a fool to deny that God hasn't done all this. He has been working with us all along, but we did not recognize His work," Neil said.

He stopped talking for a minute, then said, "This morning, when the pastor asked if anyone wanted to receive Jesus, I put up my hand and said the prayer. Next Sunday I want to go up and give my testimony."

"Neil, really? Oh! What wonderful news; praise the Lord. I'm so happy for you," I said, rejoicing that Neil now believed in my Lord.

"Neil, I know of another miracle," I added. "I know I was drawn here. The night before I got here, God gave me a vision of a little light shining bright in the middle of the darkness. At first, I did not think it was a vision, but this light has never left me. It is always with me, dispelling all the darkness, and it has gotten brighter the longer I stay here."

Neil held me close. It felt so good to have him near. I loved the evenings we spent like this.

As we were having coffee one morning a few days later, Neil said, "I'd like to take you out on an important date tonight. I've asked Wendy and Grant to come stay with the kids. What do you say?"

"Why, yes, of course. Where are you taking me? Do I get dressed up for this important date?" I asked.

"Yes, if you want. I'll pick you up at six," Neil replied. Then, he kissed me and left for work.

In late afternoon, I went to get ready, the twins busied themselves with the Lego kits Neil had bought them. I brought Amanda with me to my apartment. It pleased her to be alone with me. As I sat down to put on my makeup, she asked if she could have makeup too. Then, she wanted me to do her hair up like I had done mine. I loved having her with me. For the evening I chose a simple dark blue, short sleeve dress. Amanda said she loved it. Once I was ready, we returned to the house and were met by the twins and Neil.

"Wow, Mom, you look very pretty. Doesn't she, Dad?" little Neil said.

When I saw Neil, he was wearing black trousers, an open collar white shirt and a dark green leather jacket. It brought out the green in his eyes even more. I gave him a big smile, and before he could answer, I said, "Oh my, Neil you sure clean up nicely. And you're wearing the chain I gave you."

He smiled at me and said, "Thank you, Miss Rendell, but you look much lovelier. Are we all set to go?"

"Yes, Daddy, I'm ready," little Amanda replied, with the biggest smile on her face.

My heart just about broke when Neil picked her up and told her she was staying home with her brothers, she cried, "But I'm all pretty like Mom! Why can't I come?"

Neil put her down and said, "Tonight is just for Mom and me. But I'll take you for a ride on Rae tomorrow. Would you like that?"

Amanda nodded, she liked it when Neil paid her special attention.

Wendy came close to her and said, "Hey, Amanda, you can't leave me with all these boys. Can you show me your new baby doll?"

A very reluctant Amanda took Wendy's hand, and they headed for her room.

We said goodbye to the boys, and as I went out of the door, I noticed them giving Neil a thumbs-up.

When we got into the Jeep, I asked, "What was that about?"

"Oh, you know little boys. They think it's funny that we're going on a date," Neil replied.

Neil brought me to the finest restaurant in town. After we had a long leisurely meal, followed by coffee and dessert, Neil told me he had another surprise for me, but we would have to go back home before he could tell me what it was.

All the way home, I kept asking him, but he wouldn't tell me.

Once at the ranch, Neil drove up to the old house.

Before we got out of the Jeep, Neil said, "Trudy, I hope you like what I did. Would you like to see inside?"

"Yes, I would," I said, wondering what he was talking about. He had never mentioned he was doing anything to the house.

Neil came to help me out of the Jeep and walked me to the door. When he opened the door, I was very surprised to see all the changes.

As I walked in, I said, "Wow! This is very nice. You never told me you were doing any of this. Why didn't you tell me? You must have been working on this for a while."

"Well, yes, I have. I started on it after the clinic and hospital were finished. But I had to redraw the plans when I learned about the kids," Neil said.

As I looked around, I saw the house was totally different from the last time I had been there: the living room had a new hardwood floor, and the big stone fireplace had been cleaned up. The staircase was refurbished with new handrails. The kitchen and dining room were now across from the living room. To my surprise, Neil had kept the green appliances, and when I asked why, he said, "Because I like them. Oh, they're not the same appliances; these are brand new. What do you think?"

"Neil, it looks great. The appliances look like they belong. The entire house looks amazing," I replied.

When we went upstairs, I found that the entire space was open.

"This will be the boys' rooms. I had removable walls put in," Neil said. He went to what looked like a closet and pulled out the wall. "What do you think? Do you think the boys will like it?"

"It's different. The twins like to do things together. I think they'll love it," I replied.

"Yes, I think so too. When Ned sleeps over, there'll be room for him here too," Neil said. Then, he took my arm and said, "Come. I want to show you something else."

He led me downstairs, and to the back of the house. "I added an extension to the back. Come this way. This will be Amanda's room," Neil said as he opened the door to the room.

I looked inside the room and saw it was painted lavender. "Amanda will like this; she loves purple," I said.

Neil nodded, then he turned to go to the door on the opposite wall and said, "I need your input on how to finish this room."

He opened the door to the room, and as I stepped inside, I saw that the room was empty except for one chair in the middle of it, all decorated with wildflowers.

Neil led me to it and asked me to sit down. Standing in front of me, he went down on one knee and said, "Trudy, will you marry me? I love you. Please say yes."

Somehow, I was not surprised that he had done this. I had dreamed about it, and I had wished many times that he would propose.

I looked at Neil and said, "Yes, Neil, I'll marry you. I love you."

We kissed, then still holding me he said, "Just a minute. I have to find the ring,"

He reached over my shoulder and said, "Neil said he put it in the butter cup. Oh! There it is."

Now I was surprised and said, "Did the twins know you were going to propose?"

Before he answered he slipped the ring on my finger and kissed me again. Then, he said, "I would not have been able to do this alone. The twins helped with the flowers, although it was Amanda who picked most of them. The boys decorated the chair. It was little Neil's idea to hide the ring in the butter cup. Do you like the ring?"

I looked down at my hand and admired the ring. When I looked at the large solitaire diamond, it sparkled back at me. "Oh yes Neil! It's so beautiful! And it fits my finger perfectly. This is such a wonderful surprise. You have made me so very happy!" I said as I encircled my arms around his neck and gave him a passionate kiss. Still holding me close, he looked around the room and said, "Tell me what you want me to do with the room."

"I take it this will be the master bedroom?" I asked.

He nodded, then looking in my eyes, he asked, "You don't have to tell me right now, but I'd like to decide when we will be getting married. Do you want a long engagement?"

"No. I would like to get married as soon as Richard and Star return. Is that too quick?" I answered.

"Trudy, darling, that's why I love you so much: we think alike," Neil said as he gave me a huge hug and a kiss.

We were having supper the next evening when Neil got a call from Richard. Once he ended the call, we were all looking at him, waiting to hear what Richard had said. But Neil just sat there, not saying anything.

"Well, what did Richard say?" I asked.

He looked at us and said, "Well, Star and the baby are coming home. Richard will be coming home, then flying over to go get her and the baby. Richard also said that Star wants us to make a nursery out of the reading room. She has ordered all kinds of furniture, it should be here any day now. When that furniture comes, we might need help to put it together. Would you guys want to help?"

The twins both agreed that they would be happy to help.

Two days later, Richard brought Ned home. Before we could tell Richard about our engagement, he left us and went to be with Star. We were all very happy to see Ned home again. The twins bombarded him with all kinds of questions. It did not seem like they had anything against him.

That night, when I went to tuck Ned into bed, I said, "I'm so happy that you are home. Sounds like you had a great time with your dad."

"Yes, Mom, I did, but it's nice to be back with you and the twins."

"Ned, I have to tell you something. Uncle Neil has asked me to marry him."

"I knew it! He told me he was going to. Mom, that is so great," he said, sitting up to give me a hug.

"You knew? You have no problem with me marrying Uncle Neil?" I asked.

Ned gave me a puzzled look and said, "Of course not. It will be really great; we'll all be one big family."

A few days later, the baby furniture Star had ordered arrived. For the next week, we spent our time putting furniture together and setting up the baby's room.

Amanda was helping me put baby clothes in the dresser when she asked, "Do you think the baby will like her room?"

"Oh, I think so, but she might not notice. She'll be very small. That's why Star has been taking care of her at the hospital," I replied.

"Will she be small like my baby doll?" Amanda asked, picking up the Baby Alive doll that Neil had bought her.

"You know, I think your baby doll might be bigger than the baby," I said.

Amanda looked at her doll and said, "Really? She'll be that little? I'll help take care of her, like I take care of my dolly."

With Richard and Star coming home, I decided it was time to start planning my wedding. As Neil watched TV that evening, I started a to-do list.

Neil saw what I was doing and asked to see what I had on the list. After looking it over, he said, "I'll take care of the boys' things." He handed the list back and returned to watch his show.

"You're not going to do anything else?" I asked.

"No, that's it. You can take care of everything else. You're good at doing things like that," he replied. He must have seen the disappointment in my face, for he started to laugh and said, "Oh, darling, you know I'll do anything that needs to be done. It's our wedding, and I want it to be perfect for you. I'm just teasing. Now come here. I need a hug."

He reached out for me, so I went to sit on his lap.

"You like doing that, don't you? You're always teasing me. You'd better watch out, because two can play that game," I said, giving him a huge hug.

He returned the hug and said, "Darling, I love you."

"I love you too, but this is not planning a wedding. We don't even have a date set," I said.

"I was thinking that maybe we could set the date for the last day of August. That way, we'll know for sure that the baby will be home. Roger's rodeo circuit will be over, and he'd be home too," Neil suggested.

"Yes, that's a very good idea. I like it. That way, it will not feel like we have to rush," I replied.

Neil looked at me and said, "I wish it were sooner, but every good thing is worth waiting for."

With the date set, Neil and I set out to make an invitation on the computer. Once we had agreed on the design, I printed it out.

Neil looked it over and asked, "How many people should we invite?"

"Well, I don't know. I was thinking of inviting just the people from around here. I don't know very many people," I replied.

Neil looked at me and asked, "Don't you want any of your old friends to come?"

"Neil, I've never felt that I was close to anyone. Besides, I don't have their addresses."

"What about your family?"

"My family? Maybe my brother Andy, but he's in the air force. I don't think he would be able to come. No, I don't think any of my brothers would want to come. They're much too busy to make time for me," I replied.

15

With the wedding day fast approaching, I went to look at my wedding dress. I had hung the dress in the closet when I first moved here. It had taken me a long time before it felt right to look at it. When I finally did, it surprised me how wonderful it looked. I had returned it to the bag and had not taken it out since. Now as I took it out, I remembered the day I found the note and what it said. This was a bittersweet moment, for I knew my mother would have loved to be with me on my wedding day.

Oh, Mom, I wish you were here. I know you would love Neil and the kids, I thought.

I laid the dress on the bed and examined it. I had forgotten how beautiful it was. The dress was white silk and had a one-shoulder neckline with a strap going over the left shoulder, covered with handmade silk flowers. The flowers were larger at the top of the shoulder, and as they went down across the bodice, they gradually became smaller. The dress had a fitted bodice, and at the waist it flared out into a full skirt. As I was putting the dress back into the bag, I noticed that there was something at the bottom of it. I reached in and pulled out a piece of the same silk that my dress was made of.

I could make a dress for Amanda with this. Oh, Mom, you thought of everything, I thought as I wiped away a tear running down my cheek.

I returned the dress to the closet, then went to see if there would be enough material to make Amanda a dress. I was very pleased to find that there was enough fabric, but I would have to get some help to make the dress.

The next morning, as we were having breakfast, I told Neil about my dilemma.

Ned interjected, "Mom, you could ask Liz. She makes clothes for her twins."

"Ned, thank you so much! You just made my day. I'll go call Liz and see if she can help me," I said as I kissed Ned on the cheek.

"Can my cousins and I come? We haven't played with Trevor in a long time," Ned said.

After I made the call, I told the boys that Liz was expecting us that afternoon.

When we got there, Trevor was waiting for us, holding four water guns. I barely had the car stopped when all three boys flew out of the car.

As they raced toward Trevor, I heard Richard say, "Oh, this is going to be so much fun! A water fight!"

I had to shake my head. I would never understand the way these boys thought.

I unbuckled Amanda from her car seat and went to join Liz and her twins.

As we enjoyed the lemonade Liz offered us, I said, "Liz, it's so good of you to help me with the dress. I've never made a dress on my own before, and I don't want to do something wrong and ruin the silk material."

"Oh my! The material is silk? I've never worked with silk before. I don't know, Trudy. That's a little more than I have ever tried to do, but if you want me to help you, I will," Liz said. She took a drink of lemonade and asked, "Do you have a pattern?"

When I shook my head, she said, "You might be in luck; I just finished making my girls new dresses. We could adapt the pattern to make it fancier. Just wait here. I'll go get the pattern."

When I saw the picture on the pattern, I said, "That's just

perfect. It looks like it will be pretty, and yet it seems simple to make. Between the two of us, I think we could make it."

"Yes, I think so too. Do you sew? Because I'm not touching your material," Liz said.

"Yes, but it's your machine. My mother was a seamstress and would not let anyone use her machine. I'd prefer if you did the sewing," I replied.

"No, I want you to do the sewing. I don't want to ruin the material. How about if we cut out the pattern today, and tomorrow we can make the dress?" Liz suggested.

As we worked, Liz asked about our wedding plans and when Richard and Star would be returning home. I told her that the plans were going well, and that Richard and Star's return all depended on the baby's health.

Then, I asked, "Did you know little Amanda's mother?"

"Yes, I did. I knew Jill and her sister, Amanda. Amanda was a good friend. We did all kinds of things together. She loved growing flowers and wanted to start a gardening club, but none of the neighbors were interested in joining our club, so she gave up on that idea. When she saw the afghan I had knitted, she wanted to learn how to knit but gave up after just a few tries. I don't think she was the knitting type. I liked to be with Amanda; she liked having fun. I don't think I ever saw her unhappy. I still miss her, even after all these years. Jill was younger, I remember her as a little flirt. I never got to know her that well. She was very pretty, with blue eyes and long blonde hair. When she started flirting with Neil, I don't think he had a chance; she just charmed him. He fell head over heels in love with her. Once they were married, she caused him such agony. But, hey, I don't want to speak ill of the dead," Liz said as she finished cutting the piece for the sleeves.

"Is little Amanda like Jill?"

"Oh, she might look like Jill, but she's not at all like her. I think she's more like you than Jill or Amanda."

"How's that?"

"Little Amanda is a caring little girl. Look at her playing with the twins, she likes to play with dolls and care for them. She's a little sweetie," Liz answered.

We finished cutting out the pattern and went outside to see what the boys were doing. They were soaking wet, and when they saw us, they came running and threatened to soak us also.

"You get me wet, and you'll be sorry," Liz warned.

Trevor laughed and without a thought to what his mother had just said, shot a stream of water right at her.

"Oh, you little rat! I'll get you." She ran after him, but he got away.

He turned and said, "Ha-ha! You can't catch me."

Liz returned to the deck, and as she looked at her wet shirt, she told the boys to go play farther away from us.

It was near supper time when I got the soaking-wet boys into the car to go home. I thanked Liz for her help and told her I'd see her the following day.

The next day only Amanda and I returned to Liz's house, because Neil took the boys swimming at a nearby lake.

As I pinned the dress on Amanda, she asked, "Is this going to be my wedding dress, Mommy?"

"Yes, sweetheart. This is the dress you'll wear to my wedding. You are going to be my flower girl," I replied.

"What does a flower girl do, Mommy?" she asked.

"You will walk in front of me and drop flower petals on the floor as we walk to where Daddy will be waiting for us," I told her.

She looked at me and said, "Oh, that's easy! I can do that."

After I finished pinning the dress and helped Amanda take it off, I helped her put her clothes back on and told her to go play with Liz's twins.

Liz had the sewing machine ready, so I sat down and began to sew.

"They all call you Mom?" Liz asked.

"Oh yes, from the very first; Ned told them to. Even Neil calls me

Mom around the kids. I always thought that when I got married, it would only be me and my husband to start with. But I don't mind how it's turned out. I love them all; they're great kids," I replied.

"You are a great mother to them. Look how much Ned has changed. All those kids already love you to bits," Liz commented.

I thanked her for the kind words and continued sewing the dress.

By the time Amanda and I arrived home that afternoon, her dress was nearly completed; all I had to do was hem the skirt.

A few days later, I took Amanda to my apartment to try on the dress. She was the picture of a little princess.

She twirled around and said, "Oh, Mommy, it's so beautiful! Can I go show it to Daddy?"

"Oh, Amanda, why don't we let Daddy wait to see the dress on the wedding day? It'll be a surprise for Daddy," I replied.

"Oh, a surprise dress. Yes, Mommy; I'd like to surprise Daddy," Amanda whispered as she held her little finger to her lips.

The next morning, while we were talking about taking the boys to get their outfits for the wedding, little Amanda came to sit on Neil's lap. Amanda adored her daddy and loved to be alone with him.

"What are you going to wear to the wedding?" Neil asked her.

She looked at me and whispered, "Oh, Daddy, it's a surprise dress. Mommy said you can see it on the wedding day."

"A surprise dress?" Neil whispered back.

She nodded her head.

It made me smile to see how well they got along.

I stood up and said, "I'll leave the two of you alone. I have to go talk to Dell about some wedding plans." I met Dell in the kitchen and went over what I wanted for the banquet and what still needed to be done. Then as we finished, she said, "What about flowers? Will you have a bouquet?

"Oh, I never thought of that." Then a thought came to me and I said, "My mom liked lilies. What if I got lilies for my bouquet? I could get five lilies to represent my family who won't be here."

"Trudy, I'll take care of it. Leave it to me," Dell replied.

That afternoon, while we were at Neil's house, a car drove up. We all watched as it came to a stop and a pretty blonde lady stepped out of the car. It was Lisa, carrying a cake.

"Who is that, Dad?" little Richard asked.

Before Neil could answer, Lisa walked up the front steps.

"Hi, Dr. Neil! I made you a cake," she said as she raised it up to him for him to take.

"Why did the lady make you a cake, Dad? It's not your birthday," little Neil said.

I saw Lisa's smile fade away when she heard little Neil say, "Dad."

She looked at Neil and said, "You have kids? I thought you were single."

"Yes, Lisa, I have kids," Neil said. "Would you like to meet them?"

"Oh no, that's okay. I've got to go. Bye," Lisa replied.

She turned and returned to her car without looking back.

I couldn't help but feel sorry for her.

It was only ten days before the wedding, and Richard and Star had not returned home. I was a little concerned that they would not be back in time. They were supposed to be home two weeks ago, but the baby had a setback. On a happy note, though, Roger and Tex returned from the rodeo circuit.

Roger was so excited to see us all and couldn't wait to show everyone all the prizes he and Bud had won, especially the trophy cup they had won on the last day of competition.

Ned and the twins were amazed by all the prizes.

The day after, much to our relief, Richard called to say he and Star were coming home with the baby.

When they arrived home, we were all waiting outside for them.

Ned and Roger were very excited to see their father again. They both ran to him, and each of them hugged him. They both wanted to tell their father all about what they had done in his absence.

Richard stopped them, saying, "I missed you too, but slow down.

We must get the baby in the house first. Then, we can catch up on the news."

After Star had taken the baby out of the car, we all followed her into the house. She took the baby out of her car carrier and went to sit on the couch so that the children could have a better look at her.

All the children gathered around and stood there in awe, commenting on how little she was.

Little Amanda sat beside Star and said, "She's so little. She has dark hair, just like you have."

"Yes, she does, doesn't she?" Star said as she smiled at little Amanda.

I sat beside Amanda and asked Star if I could hold the baby.

As I held her, I said to her, "Oh my, you are so little. I've never held such a tiny baby before."

The resemblance between the baby and Star was even more striking than it had been in the photo.

As I looked at the baby, I said to Star, "Yes, she does look like you. Her eyes and mouth are very similar to yours." Then looking up at Star I continued to say, "We have the nursery all ready. I hope you'll like what we did."

"Oh, I'm sure it will be fine," Star said. She then turned to the boys and asked, "Now, boys, what did you want to tell your dad?"

After Roger and Ned had recounted their adventures, Ned said, "Uncle Neil has something to tell you too." Richard and Star both looked at Neil with a questioning look.

Neil came to sit next to me, took my hand, and said, "Trudy and I are getting married. We have everything ready. We were just waiting for you to get home."

"Oh my! Why didn't you tell us before? When is the big day?" Star asked in total surprise. When I told her the date, she added, "Trudy, Neil, I'm so happy for you two."

Richard shook his head and said, "This is just like you, Neil. Congratulations." He hugged Neil and then said, "I wish you two the best."

"Oh, but there's more," Neil said. "You are now looking at the new me. I've turned my life over to Jesus. Next Sunday, Trudy and I are going to be baptized and give our testimonies."

I saw that both Richard and Star were stunned. They both looked at us, not able to say anything for a second.

Then, looking at Richard, Star said, "I know God had His hand in this. The Lord has certainly answered our prayers."

As the conversation continued, Richard and Neil went on to talk about the ranch, while Star and I talked about the baby. The boys had no interest in any of the topics, so they went to play outside.

With all the excitement of Richard and Star returning, it took a while to get the boys to bed that night.

Amanda, on the other hand, was so tired, she had fallen asleep on Neil's lap right after supper.

Once all the kids were finally in bed and asleep, we adults met in the living room to relax and watch a little TV.

Star was feeding the baby her bottle when Neil said, "Star, I've decided who should be the baby's parents. Do you and Richard still want to adopt her?"

"Why, yes, Neil, very much," Star said with much joy in her voice.

"That's what I thought you'd say. I'm glad because I've decided the baby should be yours. You've been taking care of her like she was your own. I think this baby was meant for both of you. She even looks like you, Star," Neil said.

"Oh, Neil, you don't know how happy you have made me," Star said, her voice breaking with emotion.

"Neil, are you completely sure that this is what you want?" Richard asked.

"Yes, Richard, I'm absolutely sure about it. I've already asked a lawyer to look into doing the adoption. There is no birth certificate for her, so maybe the court might not see me as the father. You could petition the court as an uncle because Roger and Ned are her cousins by blood. But the lawyer will advise us," Neil replied.

I could see Star tearing up as she said, "Neil, thank you for doing this. The first time I saw the baby, I knew I had to care for her. I was drawn to her; it was if she were mine."

"Have you thought of a name for her?" I asked.

"Yes, we have. What do you think of Esther? It's an old biblical name; she was a lady who saved her people," Richard replied.

"It sounds all right to me. I'll advise the lawyer of her name," Neil replied.

Our wedding day arrived at last. Neil took care of the boys at his house, and I took care of Amanda at my apartment. I had a stylist come to do our hair and makeup.

When I returned to my apartment after having breakfast, I noticed my bridal bouquet on the table. The bouquet had five lilies tied up with a wide emerald green ribbon. I found it amazing that Dell would have put an emerald green ribbon in my bouquet. It was the very same color I had chosen to put on Amanda's dress and in my hair. What a wonderful surprise!

My dress and Amanda's dress were carefully hung to air out.

It was the first time Star saw the dresses, and she said, "These dresses are so beautiful. Did your mother make them?"

I explained to Star that my mother had designed and made my dress, leaving the additional fabric, which Liz and I had used to make Amanda's dress.

As Star was having her hair done, the baby started to fuss. She was in her little bassinet, so Amanda went to rock her as we had taught her to do. "Don't cry, little Star," she said as she gently rocked the bassinet.

Star and I looked at each other, and Star said, "I like that name, Amanda. Little Star is a perfect name for her. Esther can be her grown-up name."

I agreed then asked, "How did you get the name Star?"

"My mom is from France and named me Étoile, which is French for Star. When we moved here, she started to call me Star because Étoile was too hard for English people to pronounce," she replied, then said, "Oh, I have some news. Richard and I talked to Neil this morning, and he told us the lawyer called him last night and told him that the judge gave his ruling regarding the baby's paternity. He said that Neil is the legal father. So the adoption can proceed."

"Oh, that's wonderful. You and Richard must be relieved," I said, then asked. "How is Neil? Is he as nervous as I am?"

"No, he didn't seem to be. He appeared to be very cheerful, teasing the boys," Star replied.

After Amanda had her hair done, I helped her with her dress then tied an emerald green ribbon around her waist. When she looked in the mirror, she twirled around and around, and said, "Oh mommy! I'm just like a princess! Look, the ribbon is the same color as my daddy's eyes."

I gave her a big smile and said, "It sure is. Now Amanda I have to get ready. Can you go sit on the couch and wait, like a princess would?" She nodded her head and did as I asked.

I went to sit at the table so the stylist could do my hair and makeup. I had her interlace a narrow emerald green ribbon throughout my hair. Once done, Star helped me with my dress. I pinned the brooch Ned had given me, in one of the flowers close to my heart.

I took one last look in the mirror and as I turned, I saw Star looking at me, she said, "You look lovely, Trudy. The picture of a beautiful bride."

I thanked her and went to give her a hug then said, "I think we're all ready, let's go."

I handed Amanda the basket filled with flower petals, she held on to it as if it were something very precious. With Amanda carrying the basket, Star carrying the baby and me carrying my bridal bouquet, we all returned to the house and headed for the front door.

Richard was to take us to Neil's house for the ceremony. When we went outside, I was surprised to see a carriage drawn by Rae waiting for us. Richard stood beside the horse, patting his head.

"This is Neil's doing, isn't it? I thought we were going by car," I said to Richard.

"It's what Neil wanted. He said he wanted Rae to be at the wedding. Hey, I'm as surprised as you are, Trudy! Come. I'll help you into the carriage," Richard said.

After helping Star and baby in the backseat, Richard helped Amanda and me in the front. Rae took his sweet time walking to the house. Amanda stood in the front of the carriage and threw petals out as we went along. When we finally got to Neil's house, I was surprised to see all the people there, standing, waiting for us.

"Look, Mommy! There's Daddy. He looks very nice. Is it his wedding too?" Amanda asked with a puzzled look on her little face.

I smiled and said, "Yes, it is, dear," I replied, realizing that Amanda did not understand what a wedding was.

She returned my smile. I was thankful she was satisfied with the answer.

After Richard helped us off the carriage, Ned walked up to me.

"Mom, you are so beautiful!" Ned exclaimed. "You look like a queen. Wait till Uncle Neil sees you! He'll love your dress. He told me to walk you to the front steps, he'll meet us there."

I gave Ned the biggest smile and said, "Oh my, look at you! You're so handsome in that cowboy suit and those boots. I like the white hat."

After I gave him a quick kiss on the cheek, he returned my smile and took my hand. As we walked towards the front steps, Amanda walked ahead of us, throwing handfuls of petals over her head. She was having so much fun. When we got to the front steps, Neil was waiting with Roger, little Neil, and little Richard. They all wore the same type of cowboy suit and boots as Ned, but they had black cowboy hats. They were so handsome, my heart almost burst with love for them.

Neil came to me, with the biggest smile on his face, and said, "My, but you're beautiful, darling. You look stunning." He took my hand from Ned and kissed it.

I looked at him and replied, "You are one handsome cowboy, my love."

After he put my hand in the crook of his arm, we started to walk up the front steps, only to be stopped by Amanda.

"Daddy, I'm supposed to walk in front to throw flowers," she said.

Neil gave her a quick kiss on the forehead and said, "Of course you are; I just forgot."

So, with Amanda throwing the flower petals, Neil and I walked up the stairs and inside the house.

Once we were inside, Amanda turned to me and said, "Mommy, I have no more flowers. Do you have more?"

"No, sweetheart, we don't need any more flowers. I'm with Daddy now. Come stand next to me. Here you can hold my bouquet. Thank you for being my flower girl," I said handing her the bouquet.

With Ned and Amanda on my right and the twins on Neil's left, we were ready to say our vows.

The pastor from the church came to stand in front of us and asked if we were ready. When we said we were, he opened in prayer, asking God to bless our union. He asked us to join hands, and then he led us through the ceremony.

After we said our vows, we exchanged rings. As Neil was putting the ring on my finger, I felt his hand was a little shaky.

So he isn't Mr. Cool and Collected, after all, I thought, smiling to myself. I looked up at him and saw he was returning the smile.

I was so enthralled in the moment, I barely heard the pastor say, "I now pronounce you man and wife."

But I did hear the most wonderful words I had ever heard: "Please meet Mr. and Mrs. Neil Lance. Neil, you may kiss your bride."

Everyone cheered as we kissed.

As I stepped back, I saw my brother Andy. At first, I thought I was imagining things, but I looked again. Sure enough, it was Andy.

I took Neil's hand and said, "You invited my brother? But how?"

"Trudy, is it all right? Are you okay?" Neil asked with concern in his voice.

"Yes, Neil, thank you for doing that. But how did you find him? I never told you where he was," I replied.

"Well, you told me he was in the air force, and I know your last name. I just made inquiries and found him," Neil replied.

By then, Andy was standing beside me.

"Hello, Trudy. You look lovely. I'm so glad to see you so happy. I was very surprised to get your invitation," Andy said as he gave me a huge hug.

"Andy, it's such a surprise to see you. Neil never told me he had sent you an invitation," I said, returning the hug.

Then, I saw him. John was here, talking to Richard.

Andy must have noticed the change in my expression, because he said, "I told John about your wedding, Trudy. He wanted to come. I hope you're all right with that."

Before I could respond John was standing in front of me.

I reached over to him and said, "I'm so happy to see you, John. I'm so glad you came to my wedding."

"Trudy, dear, that is so good to hear. I didn't know how you would react seeing me again," John said.

"John, I understand why you did what you did. Please forgive me for the mean things I said to you," I said.

"Oh, my dear, I'm the one who has to ask for forgiveness, not you. You were in pain, and I didn't help you. After I pushed you out, I felt like a heel for a long time. Then, I decided to go look for you. That's when I found that you were here," he said.

"How did you find out?" I asked.

"Oh, I went around to motels and service stations, showing your picture. Then, one day, I talked to this lady at a motel who told me she had seen you and that you had come to this ranch for a job interview. She told me how to get here. So, I came up here and waited until I saw you. Once I knew you were all right, I just left you alone and waited to see if you would get in touch with me," John replied.

"You knew I was here all along?" I asked.

"Yes, dear, I knew. When Andy told me you were getting married, I had to come. I met Neil last night, told him how you and I parted, and asked him if he'd let me come to the wedding. When Neil told me that you had not spoken of me, I told him I'd stay in the back. When I saw how you greeted Andy, I just took a chance you'd welcome me also. Trudy, I'm so pleased you found such a good man. You look very happy. I'm so happy for you. Now enough of me; you have other guests," John said.

Once we had greeted all our guests, Neil told them to meet us at the main house, where we had a delicious meal prepared for them. We got in the carriage and rode away.

I turned to look back, and there was little Amanda, holding Roger's hand and happily waving to us with her free hand. I nudged Neil, and we both waved back.

As we rode, Neil put his arm around my shoulders and gave me a passionate kiss. "Mrs. Lance, my wife. Oh, I like the sound of that."

I cuddled up to him and said, "Yes, Neil, it does sound nice. Now I feel like I belong somewhere—that this is the place where I'm meant to be."

Neil held me and said, "Yes, my darling, it is. You are mine now and belong by my side."

I sat close to him and cherished the moment, wishing that I could somehow bottle it up to keep forever. Rae's pace was a little quicker on the way back to the main house than it had been on the way to the ceremony. We were at the house in no time at all.

When we got to the house, Neil gave Rae a treat, then told the ranch hand to take care of him. We went into the house and found that Dell had everything ready for our guests. When I stepped on the back patio, I saw it had been decorated with beautiful flowers and emerald green streamers. The aroma of the food cooking was so wonderful, I couldn't wait to eat. Dell had hired a professional cook to barbecue at our wedding.

Once everyone had arrived, Richard welcomed our guests and said, "Does everyone have a glass? I want to toast the newlyweds. I'm so happy you could come celebrate my brother's wedding to a lovely lady. It's not every day I lose my nanny and welcome her as my sister-in-law. Trudy, welcome to this family."

Richard raised his glass and said, "To Trudy and Neil."

"To Trudy and Neil," echoed the crowd.

It was so wonderful to be welcomed as Neil's wife.

Ned came to stand beside Richard and said, "To my mom, you're not our nanny anymore; you're our mom and our auntie now. I love you."

Raising his glass that was filled with raspberry juice, Ned said, "To you, Mom."

When I saw all the kids raise their glasses to me, it brought tears of happiness to my eyes.

With the toasts over, everyone was invited to find a seat, and we were finally able to enjoy the delicious barbecue of prime rib.

Neil and I went to sit with the children. Amanda was very pleased to see that Neil was sitting down, so she went to him and asked if she could sit on his lap.

We were finished eating when John and Andy came to join us.

"Who are all these children? They can't possibly be yours," John said.

"John, Ned is my son; the twin boys and the little girl are Neil's," I replied.

I had to laugh when I saw how surprised he looked.

"How did that come about?" he asked.

"Well, my children are from my first marriage. Ned is Richard's son. Trudy adopted him," Neil told John, then he turned to the children and said, "Guys, this is Trudy stepdad and her brother Andy."

"Does that mean we have a grandfather?" little Neil asked.

"You bet it does. I'm very pleased to meet you all. But you all look alike; how am I going to tell you apart?" John said with a laugh.

We were still laughing when I saw Liz enter the patio, rolling in a small table with a lovely wedding cake on it. She invited Neil and me to come cut the cake.

As I came to stand closer to the cake, I saw that it had three tiers. In the middle of the top of the cake there was a figurine of a cowboy kissing his bride. The figurine was surrounded by little icing flowers of all colors. The flowers seemed to overflow the top and slip down the first tier and onto the second.

"Liz, you did this for us? Thank you, so much. It's lovely," I said, hugging her.

"Yes, Trudy. It was a joy to make. Here, Neil, help Trudy cut the cake," Liz replied as she handed Neil a knife.

We sliced into the beautiful cake and cut a piece out.

Once Neil and I each had a slice of cake, Liz said she would make sure all the guests had one.

After we finished eating our cake, Neil and I went to chat with our guests. We were talking with Andy, near the edge of the fir trees, when I felt a nudge against my back. I turned to see what it was, jumping back when I saw it was Rae.

Neil saw his horse, grabbed his bridle, and asked, "What are you doing here, Rae?"

Rae came closer to me, sniffed my dress, and let out a soft mumble.

I patted his soft nose and asked, "You like my dress?"

The horse nodded his head and gave another soft mumble.

I saw the ranch hand coming to take the horse, but before the man reached us, I said, "Neil, Rae came to see us. He wants to be part of our wedding. Let him stay."

Neil looked at the horse and said, "You can stay, but you'd better behave."

Neil looked at me, with a big smile on his face, he said, "I see you're already spoiling him. He'll think he can get anything he wants when you're around."

"Thank you, Neil," I said.

Neil let go of Rae's bridle.

As we were returning to our guests, I saw Rae go down on his front knees and bow to Neil. It amazed me how this horse always knew what was going on.

Neil smiled and said, "Oh, you are such a cad. Stop showing off."

"He's thanking you too," I said with a laugh in my voice.

When I turned to continue our chat with Andy, I found that John had joined us. He had come to take a closer look at the horse.

"John, I never knew you liked horses," I said.

"Oh, I never had much to do with them. I'm more of a truck guy. But this guy is a little different from other horses," he replied.

"Do you still have your truck?" I asked.

"Yes, I sure do. And I have a new lady in my life," John replied.

"You what?" I asked, making sure I had heard him right.

He smiled broadly at me and said, "I'm dating Mary, the lady who helped your mother. She likes coming on road trips with me."

"But Mary's a Christian," I said. "John, what happened to your notion about people like that?"

"Trudy, after your mother died, I had to reevaluate my thinking. After you left, I was all alone. Over time I noticed that Mary would walk pass my house every other day. When I saw her walk by one day, I went outside and invited her for coffee; I wanted to thank her for taking care of Ellen and apologize for the way I had spoken to her at the funeral. I was also very curious about why she had come to help your mother. I asked her about her faith. Much to my surprise, she was able to answer most of my questions. I found her to be a very lovely lady," he replied.

"So are you a believer now?" I asked.

His facial expression told me he had not expected that question.

But then, with the biggest grin on his face, John said, "A believer?

In God? Yes, Trudy, I am a Christian. I tried to resist, but after a while, I just knew that what Mary said was right."

"Oh, Dad, I'm so glad. Now my family is complete," I said, giving him the biggest hug I had ever given him.

After the hug, he took my hands in his and said, "Trudy, Andy and I have to go. I'm glad we had this talk."

"Yes, Dad, I'm glad we did too. Please come visit us very soon," I said. Turning to Andy, I added, "You too." Then I gave them both a kiss on the cheek and a big hug.

After they left, I spent the rest of the afternoon talking to our guests.

The kids loved having Rae there. They kept feeding him handfuls of grass. Little Amanda adored him; she even gave him some wedding cake. It was clear that Rae enjoyed the attention.

Neil came to my side late that afternoon and asked if I would meet him at my apartment.

I looked at him and smiled, saying, "But, honey, we still have guests here. What do you have in mind?"

He smiled back and took my hand. "You'll see, darling."

When we got to the apartment, I saw this new outfit laid out on my bed. I picked up the jacket, feeling the soft leather against my fingers. The jacket was pale beige and had an image of a bucking horse on the back, all in rhinestones of varying colors. The pants were the same shade of beige, with rhinestones going down the sides.

"Neil, this is beautiful. When did you find time to get this?" I asked, surprised to see such an outfit.

He turned me around and started to undo the buttons on the back of my dress, saying, "You can't wear this dress to the place I'm taking you." Once he had undone all the buttons, he kissed the back of my neck, sending a shiver of pleasure all the way through me.

I turned to face him and asked, "Where are we going, Honey?"

As I stepped out of the dress, he said, "Put on the outfit. I want to see how it fits."

I dressed and then went to stand in front of him.

"What do you think?" I asked. "I think it fits just right."

"Yes, it does. Now you're ready," he said, looking me over, up and down. Then, he winked at me and said, "On second thought, maybe we'll just stay here."

He took me in his arms, and we kissed.

As we finished the kiss, I asked, "Neil, what did you have in mind?"

"Trudy, I thought it would be lovely if we rode off into the sunset together and went to the place where we spent our first night together. That is where I first fell in love with you. I thought it would be a good place to start our marriage and life together. What do you think?"

"We're going to the shack? But we'll have to cross the creek. Oh, Neil, I don't know about this," I said, alarmed that I would have to see the creek again.

"Darling, do you trust me? It will be okay, I promise," Neil said, looking deep into my eyes.

"Yes, Neil, my love. I do trust you; I would go anywhere with you. I know you would never put me in a place that would harm me," I replied as I embraced him.

Then, pulling away slightly, I said, "Neil, I'll need some things to take with me. I'll just go—"

Before I could finish, he said, "Trudy, all you will need is already at the shack. Wendy and Grant took care of everything. Now, come on. Let's go."

When we returned to the patio at the main house, I was surprised no one was there, but I could hear the sound of voices inside the house. We went inside, only to find that everyone was waiting for us to return. Neil led me to the front door, where Rae and Bell were waiting for us.

I gave all the boys kisses and hugs and made them promise to be good for Star.

When I came to give Amanda a kiss, she said, "Mommy, am I going with you and daddy? It's my wedding too."

When Neil heard what she said, he went to pick her up.

"Amanda, tonight is just for Mommy and me. Besides, who's going to help Star with the baby? We'll be back in two sleeps," Neil said, hugging her.

"Two sleeps? Okay, Daddy, but just two sleeps," Amanda replied, holding up two little fingers.

Neil put her down, then turned toward me.

Before Amanda had time to think more about the arrangements, Neil said to me, "Come, darling, let's go."

Neil helped me onto Bell, then he got on Rae.

When I turned to wave goodbye, Roger was holding little Amanda's hand, Ned and the twins stood together, close by her, happily waving back. When I saw them all together, it brought such joy to my heart.

When I looked back at Neil, he took my hand and gave me the biggest smile.

Then, together, we rode off into the sunset and into our bright future. For I knew the Light was with us.

Printed in the United States
By Bookmasters